Learn to Draw
PRINCESSES

Disney princesses can be found in a fairy-tale castle, an enchanted wood, the French countryside, a desert kingdom—even under the sea! Although their stories may be similar—overcoming problems to reach "happily ever after"—each princess brings something special to her tale. Over the years, that "something special" has changed, but the beauty and love that shine in each princess have always remained the same.

Written by
Catherine McCafferty

Getting Started

sharpener

graphite pencil
and paper

Tools and Materials

You'll want to gather a few simple supplies to create your own Disney Princesses world. Try starting with a graphite pencil, so you can easily erase any mistakes (don't forget to grab an eraser, too!). Then you can add color with markers, crayons, colored pencils, watercolors, or acrylic paints. It's up to you!

eraser

felt-tip
markers

paintbrush
and paints

How to Use This Section

You can draw any princess by following the simple steps in this guide. You'll be amazed at how fun and easy drawing can be!

Step 1
Start your drawings in the middle of your paper so you don't run out of room.

Step 2
Each new step appears in blue, so draw all the blue lines you see.

Step 3
Refine the lines of your drawing and add the details.

Step 4
Darken the lines you want to keep and erase the rest.

colored pencils

Step 5
Add some beautiful colors to make your drawing really come alive!

Snow White

Snow White is a beautiful young princess who is badly mistreated by her wicked stepmother, the Queen. When creating Snow White, Walt Disney decided to make his first feature princess look more like a pretty "girl next door" than like a glamorous princess. Snow White does have rose-red lips, ebony hair, and skin as white as snow, which win her the title of "fairest one of all." But her rounded face and figure also show her youth and innocence.

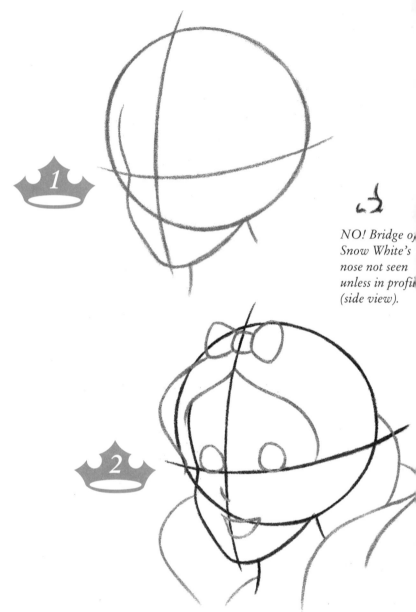

NO! Bridge of Snow White's nose not seen unless in profile (side view).

Snow White's hair is drawn with soft curves.

Eyelashes curl out from her eyelids.

Top lip is thinner than bottom lip.

Lips are soft and not too full.

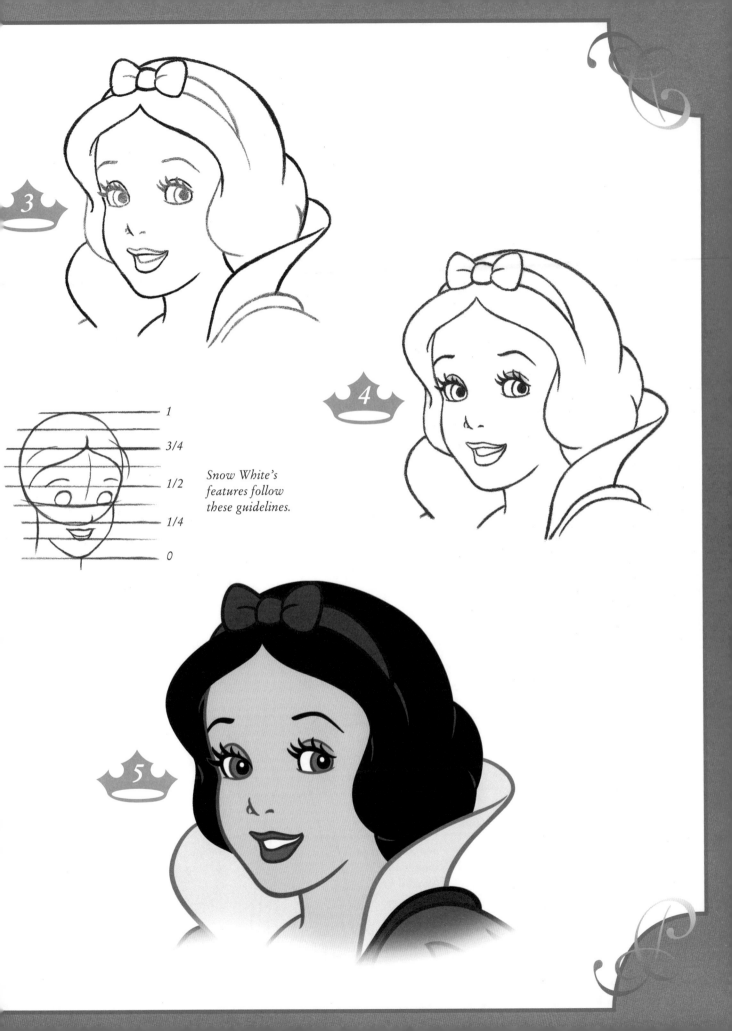

Snow White's features follow these guidelines.

Snow White

Even when she's abandoned in the forest, Snow White's kindness shines through and wins her the friendship of all the forest animals—as well as the love and loyalty of all of the Seven Dwarfs. When you draw Snow White, be sure to show the soft, sweeping lines of her dress and the gentle arm movements that emphasize her cheerful, sweet disposition and joy for life.

Snow White's hands are rounded and soft like this . . .

. . . not sharp and pointed like this.

Draw the legs as a guide, even though they're covered by a skirt.

YES! Skirt is wider than hips.

NO! Skirt is too close to hips.

Feet are small and delicate.

Snow White
is about 6
heads tall

Lines are graceful,
with no sharp angles.

NO! not angular

Figure is
rounded.

NO! not
too curvy

Cinderella

Cinderella's story seems much like Snow White's at first: Cinderella is treated badly by her stepfamily, but she overcomes all to win the love of a prince. She is also as pretty as can be, whether she appears as a simple house maiden with her hair pulled back or as a glamorous ball guest with her hair swept up. Still, Cinderella is a very different kind of princess than Snow White is. Whereas Snow White wishes and waits for her love to appear, Cinderella wills her dreams to come true, and she goes to find her Prince Charming at the ball.

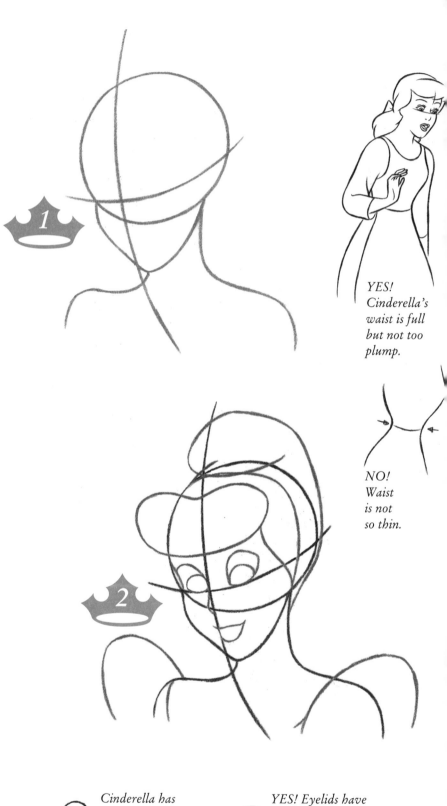

1

2

YES! Cinderella's waist is full but not too plump.

NO! Waist is not so thin.

Cinderella has almond-shaped eyes.

YES! Eyelids have slight S-curve.

NO! Not droopy—avoid sad eyes.

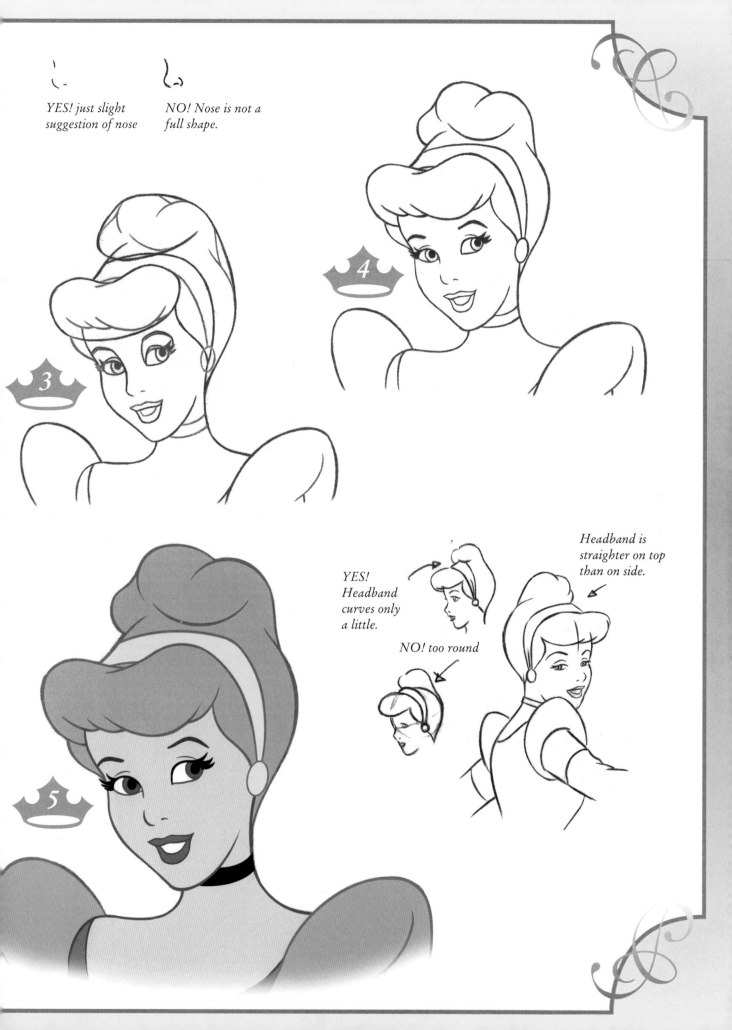

YES! just slight suggestion of nose

NO! Nose is not a full shape.

YES! Headband curves only a little.

NO! too round

Headband is straighter on top than on side.

Cinderella

Cinderella's beauty and graceful movements are evident as she runs down the stairs in her simple, homemade gown, but they are even more obvious at the ball. When she first arrives in her gorgeous dress (thanks to her Fairy Godmother), she immediately attracts everyone's attention, including Prince Charming's. When you draw her sweeping gown with billowing curves, show just a bit of the elegant lace underneath.

Cinderella's fingers are long and slender.

YES! Angles a soft and smooth.

NO! Angles a not shar

Cinderella is about 6½ heads tall.

Sleeping Beauty

Though sixteen-year-old Princess Aurora has been gifted with beauty, she looks very different from both Snow White and Cinderella. She appears older—more like a woman than a young girl. Princess Aurora spends the early years of her life in the forest as the "peasant" Briar Rose, where she wears a simple dress and holds back her wavy, waist-length hair with a headband. This is how she looks when she first meets Prince Phillip.

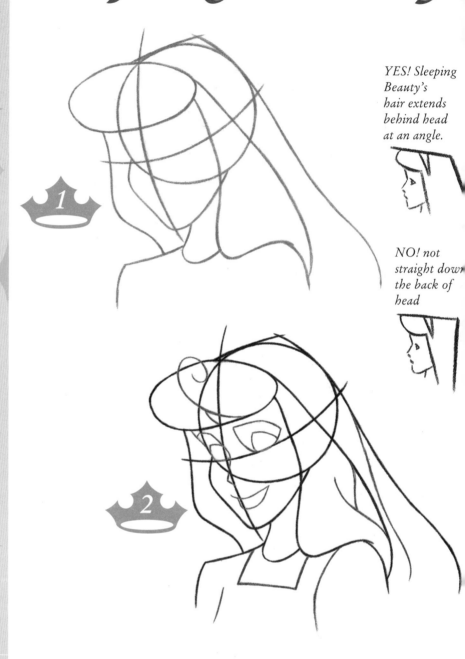

YES! Sleeping Beauty's hair extends behind head at an angle.

NO! not straight down the back of head

Eyes tilt up slightly.

YES! Eyes end pointed corners and have one thick eyelash.

NO! Not round—don't draw individua lashes.

*Top of head is
fairly flat.*

point here

*Sleeping Beauty's
features are more
angular than
Snow White's or
Cinderella's.*

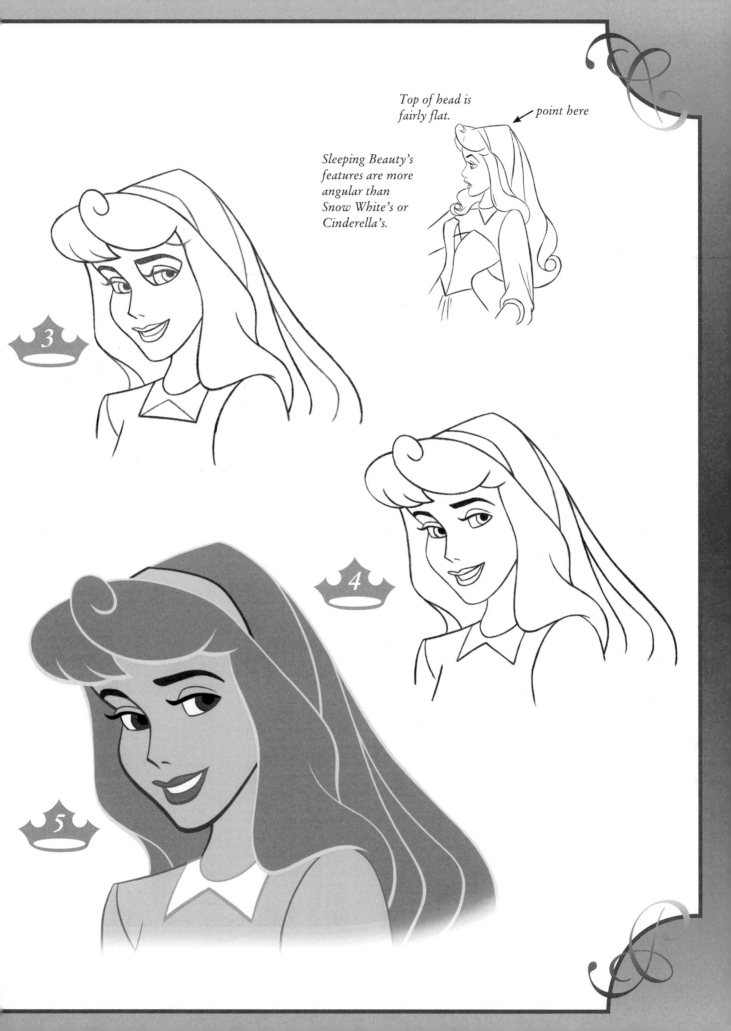

3

4

5

Sleeping Beauty

When Aurora is awakened from her sleep by a kiss from Prince Phillip, she is saved from the curse placed upon her at birth—and she gets to marry her true love! Now when she dances with her prince in the palace, her simple dress is exchanged for a lovely gown, and a beautiful tiara replaces her plain headband. Use long, slightly curved lines for her skirt to show how regal this princess has become.

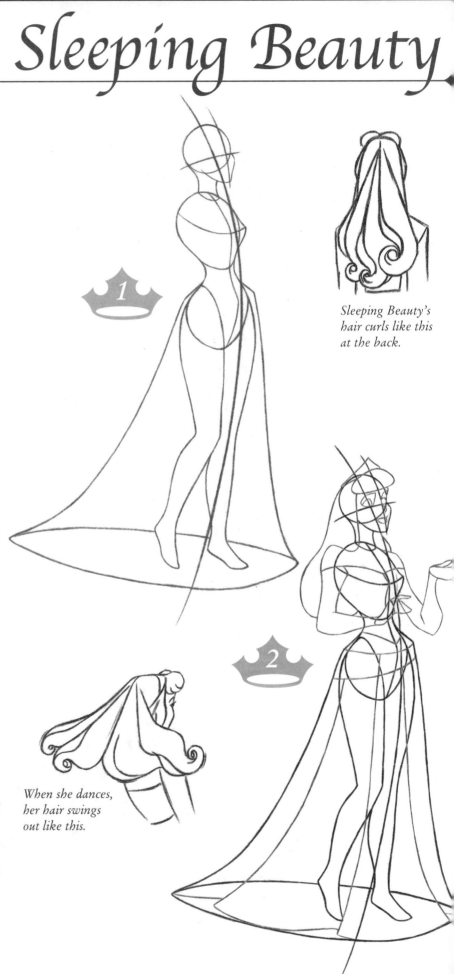

Sleeping Beauty's hair curls like this at the back.

When she dances, her hair swings out like this.

3

4

5

Sleeping Beauty
is about 6½
heads tall.

aist is
ry slim.

large bangs
on left

big curl
on right

YES! Curls
are closed,
like this.

NO! curls
not open

Ariel

In many ways, *The Little Mermaid*'s Ariel starts out as a very different character from Snow White, Cinderella, or Aurora. She is a confident, headstrong, and passionate teenager who knows exactly what she wants—and will do anything to get it. In fact, she is a princess among princesses, with no fewer than six royal sisters! Ariel lives with her sisters and her father, King Triton, under the sea in Atlantica. And her wavy red hair—a new hair color for a Disney Princess—flows with the currents in her underwater kingdom.

YES! Ariel's bangs pouf out over her forehead.

NO! Hair doesn't cover her face.

YES! Ariel's eyes are wedge-shaped.

NO! not triangular . . .

. . . nor round

hair billows out, especially underwater

YES! Lips are smooth curves.

NO! There no "dimple on top lip.

Each eyebrow is
one thin line.

YES! thin
eyebrows

NO! not thick

YES! Oval nose is
angled like this.

NO! not
horizontal
like this

Ariel

Ariel probably changes the most of all of the princesses—physically, at least. To get her prince, she trades her voice for legs and feet so she can live on land. But even without speaking, she's able to win the heart of Prince Eric. Try drawing her as we first meet her, wearing her seashell mermaid outfit and swimming freely under the sea.

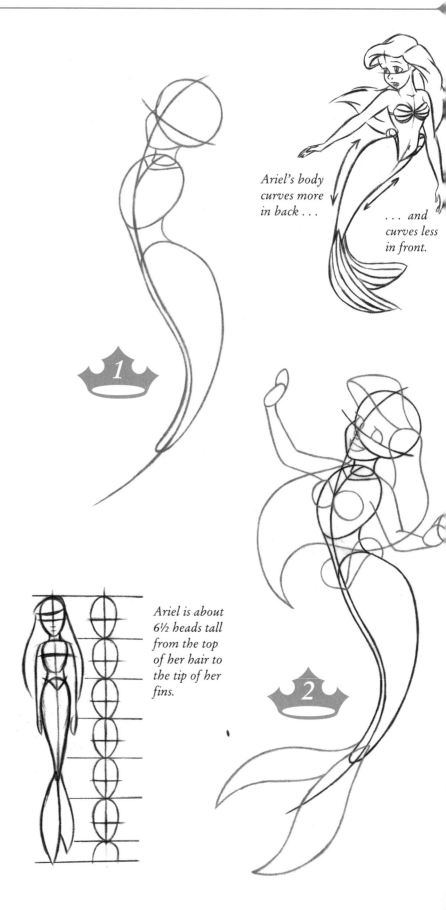

Ariel's body curves more in back . . .

. . . and curves less in front.

Ariel is about 6½ heads tall from the top of her hair to the tip of her fins.

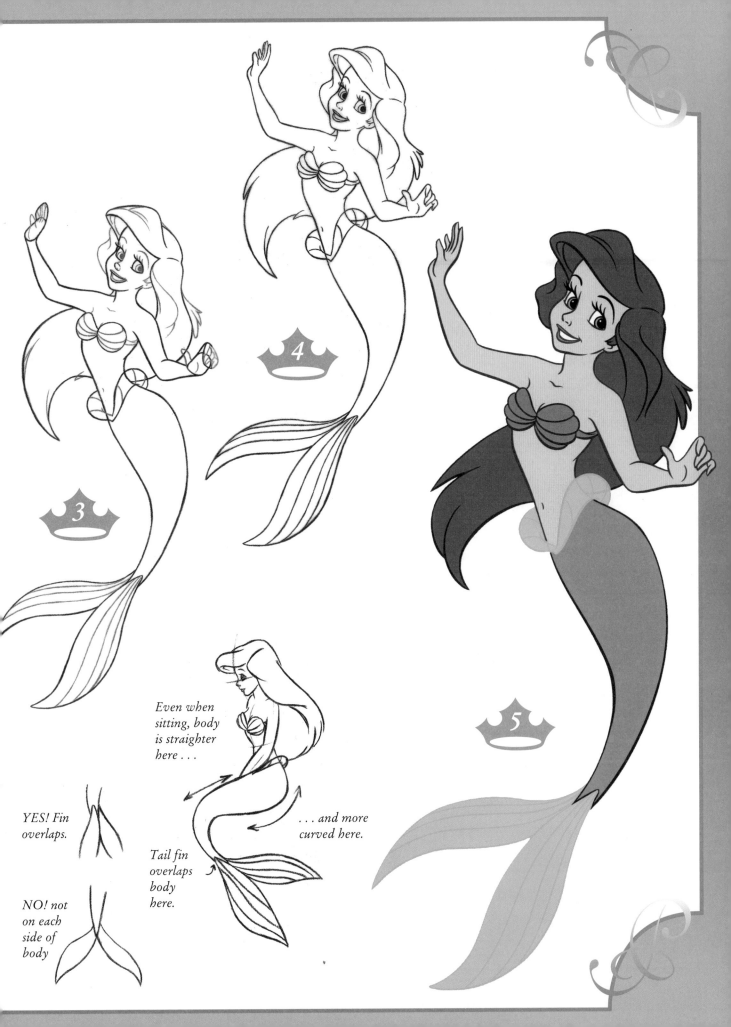

Even when sitting, body is straighter here . . .

. . . and more curved here.

Tail fin overlaps body here.

YES! Fin overlaps.

NO! not on each side of body

Belle

Beauty and the Beast's Belle may like to read and daydream about princes and princesses, but she doesn't live the life of royalty. And she certainly isn't looking for a prince—especially if the closest thing to a "prince" in her town is the conceited Gaston! Down-to-earth Belle keeps her brown hair pulled back in a simple ponytail while leading a "normal life" in her small, provincial town. Her large, almond-shaped eyes capture the sense of wonder and excitement she feels about new ideas and places.

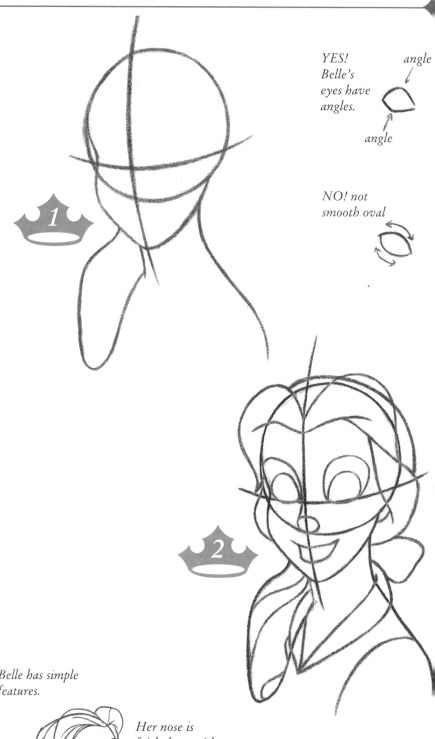

YES! Belle's eyes have angles.

angle

angle

NO! not smooth oval

Belle has simple features.

Her nose is fairly long with a defined bridge.

thin upper lip

YES! Upper lip is thinner than lower lip.

NO! not even sizes

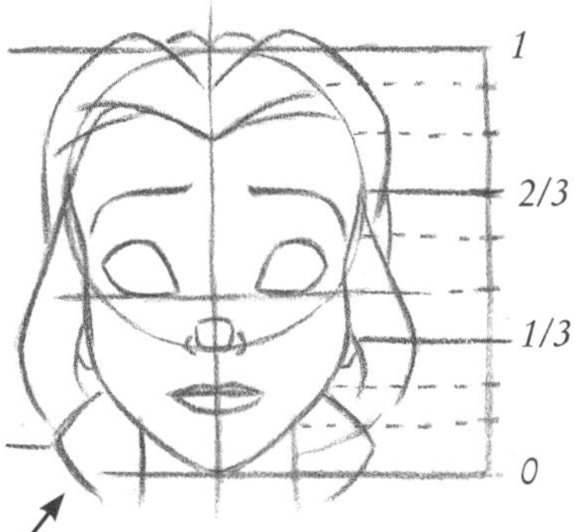

Belle's facial features follow these guidelines.

1

2/3

1/3

0

YES! Eyebrows are smooth and thin.

NO! not thick or angular

Hair bow extends beyond chin line.

4

3

5

When eyes close, angle is less dramatic.

Belle

Belle's prince is horrifying at first—a handsome man trapped in the body of a hideous-looking beast. But Belle soon warms up to his gentle nature, and when she prepares to join the Beast for dinner, she dresses in a beautiful ball gown and wears a hairstyle befitting a princess. Draw Belle in her elegant, yellow gown, ready to waltz with the Beast in the grand ballroom.

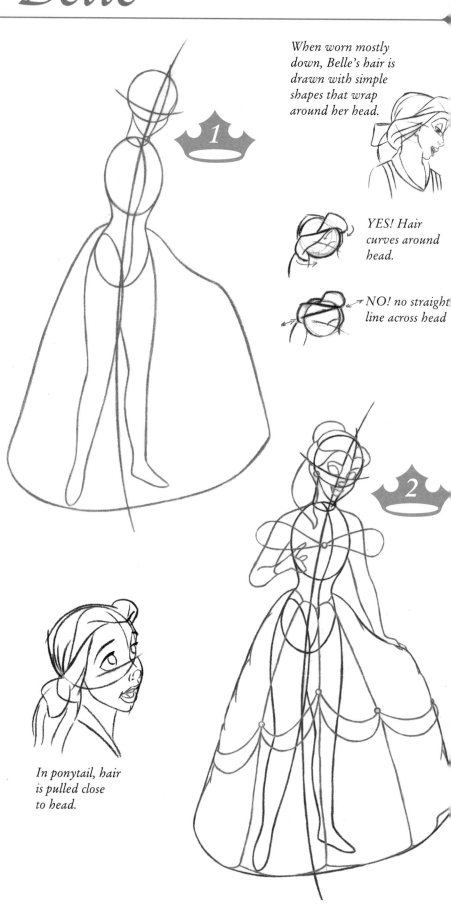

When worn mostly down, Belle's hair is drawn with simple shapes that wrap around her head.

YES! Hair curves around head.

NO! no straight line across head

In ponytail, hair is pulled close to head.

*Belle is about
6½ heads tall.*

Jasmine

Like Aurora, *Aladdin*'s Jasmine is about to have her fateful sixteenth birthday at the beginning of her story. But while Aurora's fairy "aunts" keep hopeful princes away, Jasmine's father hopes that his daughter will marry one of the many princes who come to see her. But Jasmine has other ideas. She would rather marry for love—and she chooses the handsome, young street thief, Aladdin. Jasmine's dramatic features emphasize her exotic beauty, making her unique among the Disney Princesses.

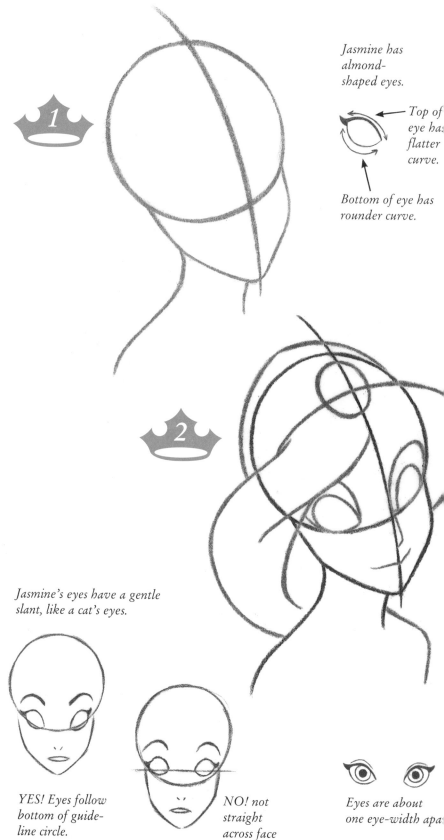

Jasmine has almond-shaped eyes.

Top of eye has flatter curve.

Bottom of eye has rounder curve.

Jasmine's eyes have a gentle slant, like a cat's eyes.

YES! Eyes follow bottom of guide-line circle.

NO! not straight across face

Eyes are about one eye-width apart

*hick
eyebrows*

*Hair overlaps
eyebrows.*

ll bottom lip

*YES! Back of hair
comes out to soft
point.*

*NO! not round;
not so small*

Jasmine

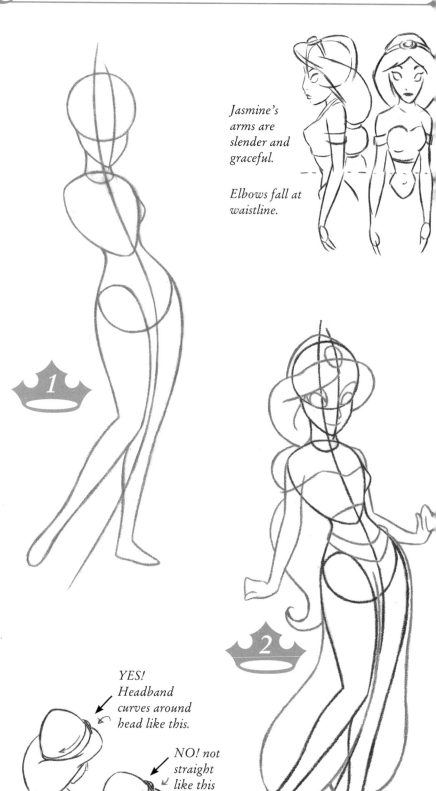

Jasmine's arms are slender and graceful.

Elbows fall at waistline.

Jasmine's outfit gives her the freedom and flexibility to move quickly—whether she is running away from Aladdin (posing as Prince Ali) or from the evil Jafar. But she looks just as graceful as the other princesses do in their fancy ball gowns, and every bit a princess. Be sure to draw the sparkling jewel in her headband and the curled toes of her delicate slippers.

YES! Headband curves around head like this.

NO! not straight like this

Jasmine is just a little more than five heads tall.

Mulan

This plucky heroine is a
study in contrasts. Mulan is
graceful, yet feisty; respectful,
yet defiant. Behind her classic
Asian features lies a quick
mind—and she's not afraid
to speak it. Animators had to
show both the outwardly
traditional Mulan and her bold
inner spirit. They chose to
create her character using
simple shapes and few details.
Her clean, down-to-earth look
emphasizes that she just wants
to be true to herself. As
you draw Mulan, focus on
simplicity, shape, and
proportion.

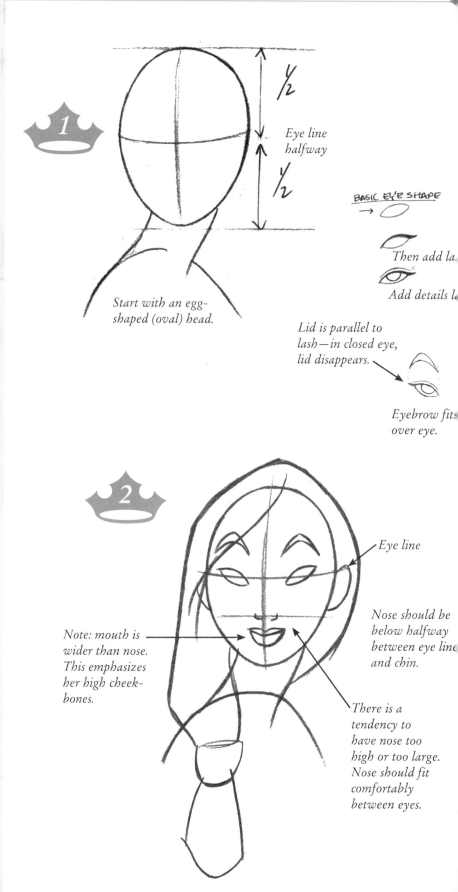

1

$\frac{1}{2}$

Eye line
halfway

$\frac{1}{2}$

Start with an egg-
shaped (oval) head.

BASIC EYE SHAPE
→

Then add la...

Add details l...

Lid is parallel to
lash—in closed eye,
lid disappears.

Eyebrow fits
over eye.

2

Eye line

Nose should be
below halfway
between eye line
and chin.

Note: mouth is
wider than nose.
This emphasizes
her high cheek-
bones.

There is a
tendency to
have nose too
high or too large.
Nose should fit
comfortably
between eyes.

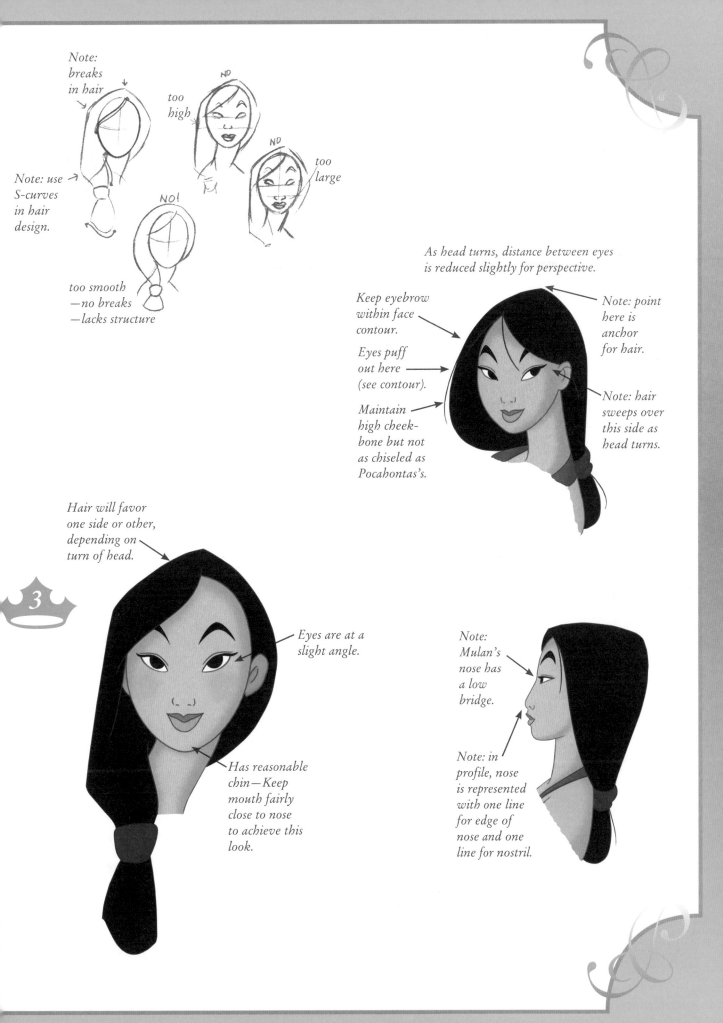

Note: breaks in hair

Note: use S-curves in hair design.

too high

NO

too large

NO

NO!

too smooth
—no breaks
—lacks structure

As head turns, distance between eyes is reduced slightly for perspective.

Keep eyebrow within face contour.

Eyes puff out here (see contour).

Maintain high cheek-bone but not as chiseled as Pocahontas's.

Note: point here is anchor for hair.

Note: hair sweeps over this side as head turns.

Hair will favor one side or other, depending on turn of head.

3

Eyes are at a slight angle.

Has reasonable chin—Keep mouth fairly close to nose to achieve this look.

Note: Mulan's nose has a low bridge.

Note: in profile, nose is represented with one line for edge of nose and one line for nostril.

Mulan becomes a soldier to save her elderly father's life. She defies tradition, doing what she believes is right. The film's artists have followed her daring lead and treated her "soldier" look with an unconventional approach. Her basic features are the same, but slight changes have been made to help hide her femininity. Here are some secrets to drawing Mulan as a soldier:

Chest is same as head volume. There is a tendency to make head too large.

Not chesty, but still retains shape.

Map out pose first, then compensate armor to fit.

Use long, flowing shapes. Worry about getting shape to work first, then worry about details. Keep shapes graceful.

As bun moves, check leading edges.

Keep in min Mulan is sti female whe she dresses u as a man.

Don't let armo stiffen pose.

Show some thickness of hair.

higher pt. than front

Remember: hair is not stiff. Bun will move with flow of action.

S-curve shallow bridge

Eye is close to nose.

Watch space here.

Remember: nose shouldn't stick out too much.

Note: has slight overbite.

too wide

too small

NO

NO! TOO FLAT

YES

some dimension

too stiff

Remember flow and simplicity.

3

Even in armor, need to retain graceful, pleasing shapes.

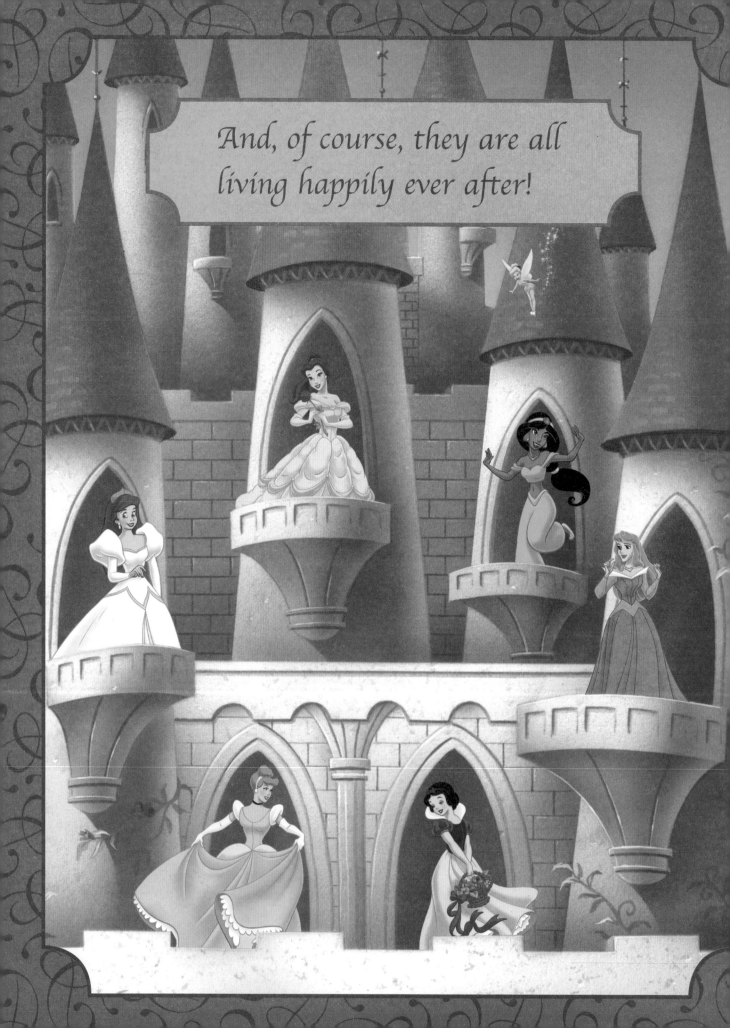

And, of course, they are all living happily ever after!

THE PRINCESS AND THE FROG

Illustrated by Scott Tilley, Olga T. Mosqueda, and The Disney Storybook Artists

Written by Laura Uyeda

Designed by Shelley Baugh

Project Editor: Rebecca J. Razo

On a balmy New Orleans evening, two girls listen intently to their favorite fairytale about a frog wh
needs a princess's kiss to become a prince again. Charlotte says she would kiss a frog in a heartbeat i
she could marry a prince. But Tiana says she would never kiss a frog! She has other plans.

Tiana's father, James, shares his dream of opening his own restaurant one day with Tiana. He
encourages Tiana to wish upon the Evening Star, but he adds that it will take hard work to make he
dreams come true.

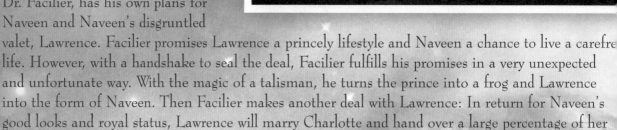

The years go by, and Tiana works
day and night, saving all of her
money to open up her father's dream
restaurant. And when the fun-loving,
carefree Prince Naveen of Maldonia
arrives in New Orleans, Charlotte
finally sees an opportunity to marry
a prince.

However, the evil voodoo man,
Dr. Facilier, has his own plans for
Naveen and Naveen's disgruntled
valet, Lawrence. Facilier promises Lawrence a princely lifestyle and Naveen a chance to live a carefre
life. However, with a handshake to seal the deal, Facilier fulfills his promises in a very unexpected
and unfortunate way. With the magic of a talisman, he turns the prince into a frog and Lawrence
into the form of Naveen. Then Facilier makes another deal with Lawrence: In return for Naveen's
good looks and royal status, Lawrence will marry Charlotte and hand over a large percentage of her
fortune to him.

Charlotte's father, Eli "Big Daddy" LaBouff, hosts an extravagant masquerade ball at his mansion.
During the ball, Charlotte meets "Prince Naveen" (the transformed Lawrence) while Tiana meets an

is instantly repulsed by the real Naveen—in
his frog form. When Tiana reluctantly kisses
Naveen, something unexpected happens…sh
transforms into a frog herself!

Both frogs flee to the bayou where they mee
a trumpet-playing alligator named Louis and
a helpful firefly named Ray. Louis and Ray
help Tiana and Naveen escape from frog
hunters and get to the powerful priestess
Mama Odie. They hope Mama Odie can us
her good magic to transform them back into humans. During their journey, Naveen teaches Tiana
how to have fun, and Tiana teaches Naveen how to work hard. They finally begin to understand and
appreciate one another.

Mama Odie explains that knowing what you need is more important than knowing what you want. Tiana fails to understand Mama Odie's important lesson. Naveen, however, starts to understand. As he looks at Tiana, he begins to realize that she is what he truly needs.

Knowing the two frogs have to figure things out for themselves, Mama Odie instructs Naveen to kiss Charlotte, the "princess" of Mardi Gras, before midnight. Then both frogs will become human again.

When Tiana isn't looking, Facilier's evil shadows swoop down and take Naveen prisoner. Facilier needs Naveen to keep his magical talisman working on Lawrence. Naveen manages to escape and climbs to the top of the Mardi Gras float to expose Lawrence and get to Charlotte. Ray snatches the talisman and takes it to Tiana. But Facilier shows up and steps on Ray. Having run off with the talisman, Tiana is unaware that Ray is hurt. Facilier quickly tracks down Tiana and corners her. He uses his magic to create a mirage of her dream restaurant and her father. Facilier says she can give her daddy everything he ever wanted—all she has to do is hand over the talisman.

"My Daddy never did get what he wanted, but he had what he needed. He had love," Tiana says. She smashes the talisman to the ground. The shadows descend upon Facilier and he vanishes into thin air, never to be seen again.

Naveen promises to marry Charlotte if she kisses him, but she must help Tiana buy the restaurant. Naveen and Tiana confess their love for each other. Upon hearing this, Charlotte agrees to kiss Naveen—not for herself but for Tiana.

But the clock strikes midnight, and it is too late. Charlotte is no longer the "princess" of Mardi Gras, so Naveen and Tiana both remain frogs. But Naveen and Tiana couldn't be happier because they're together and they're in love. Louis shows up carrying a very weak Ray. Everyone huddles around the firefly as his light flickers out for the last time.

Filled with grief, Tiana, Naveen, and Louis take Ray home to the bayou. They place him in a small leaf boat and let him disappear into the mist. Moments later, a new star shines besides the Evening Star. Ray is finally with his Evangeline.

Soon thereafter, the two frogs get married in the bayou, and they kiss. Then, in a swirl of magic, they become human! As soon as Naveen married Tiana, she became a princess—and with her kiss they both became human again.

After their wedding, Tiana and Naveen open up "Tiana's Palace"—Tiana's dream restaurant. The restaurant is everything that Tiana ever wanted, and her true love is everything she ever needed.

Tools and Materials

You'll need only a few simple supplies to create the characters from *The Princess and the Frog*. You may prefer working with a drawing pencil to begin with, and it's always a good idea to have a pencil sharpener and an eraser nearby. When you've finished drawing, you can add color with felt-tip markers, colored pencils, watercolors, or acrylic paint. The choice is yours!

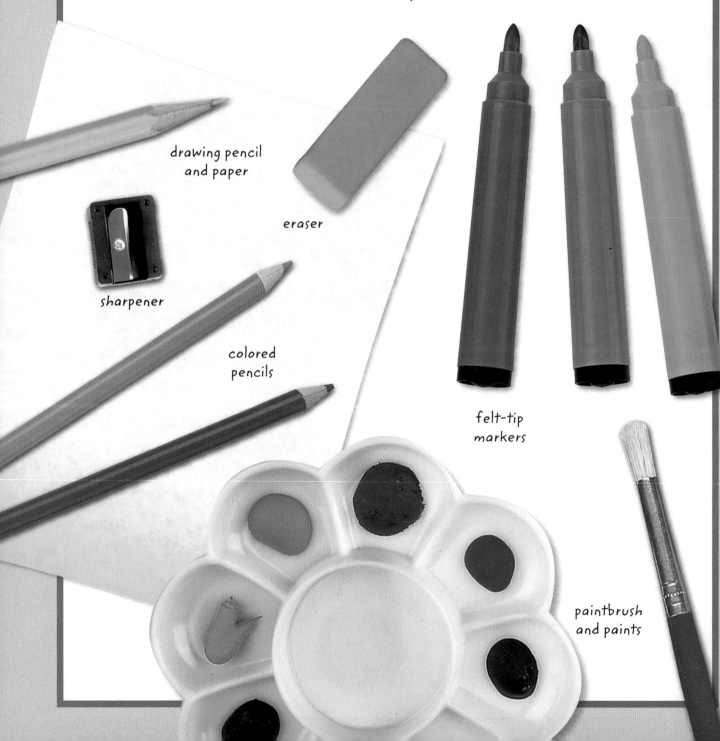

drawing pencil and paper

eraser

sharpener

colored pencils

felt-tip markers

paintbrush and paints

How to Use This Section

In this guide you'll learn how to draw Tiana and all of her friends in just a few simple steps. You'll also get lots of helpful tips and useful information from Disney artists that will help guide you through the drawing process. With a little practice, you'll soon be producing successful drawings of your very own!

First draw the basic shapes using light lines that will be easy to erase.

Each new step is shown in blue, so you'll know what to add next.

Follow the blue lines to draw the details.

Now darken the lines you want to keep, and erase the rest.

Use some magic (or crayons or markers) to add color to your drawing!

Tiana

Even as a child, Tiana is bold and spirited. She makes it quite clear to Charlotte that she would *never* kiss a frog to find her prince charming! Tiana learns from her parents that if she works hard, she can accomplish anything she sets her mind to.

1

2

3

4

Start drawing Tiana's head with a circle, then add her chin, cheeks, and ears.

Indicate wavy lines.

Note how many tendrils Tiana has.

YES! Top lip is drawn as one shape

full bottom lip

NO!

Tiana has small shoes.

Charlotte

As the richest little girl in New Orleans, Charlotte gets everything her heart desires—dolls, dresses, kittens, and puppies. And she will do just about anything to marry a prince and become a princess...even if it means kissing a frog!

1

2

3

full eyelashes

4

Head shape is carved away from a circle.

The nose is based on a triangle.

Shape of head resembles an upside-down ice cream cone.

Eudora

Eudora is Tiana's kind and nurturing mother and the most talented seamstress in New Orleans. When Tiana grows up and juggles multiple jobs, Eudora worries that her daughter is working too hard to achieve her dream. She wants Tiana to find love, be happy, and have a family of her own.

HAIR SHAPES

round
flat
part
round

round flat part
round

YES! Eyes should be almond-shaped.

NO! not too round

James

James is Tiana's father who once had a dream of opening his own restaurant. He believed that food not only brings smiles to peoples' faces, it also brings people from all walks of life together. Tiana takes after her father in many ways—she has his strength, warmth, and generosity.

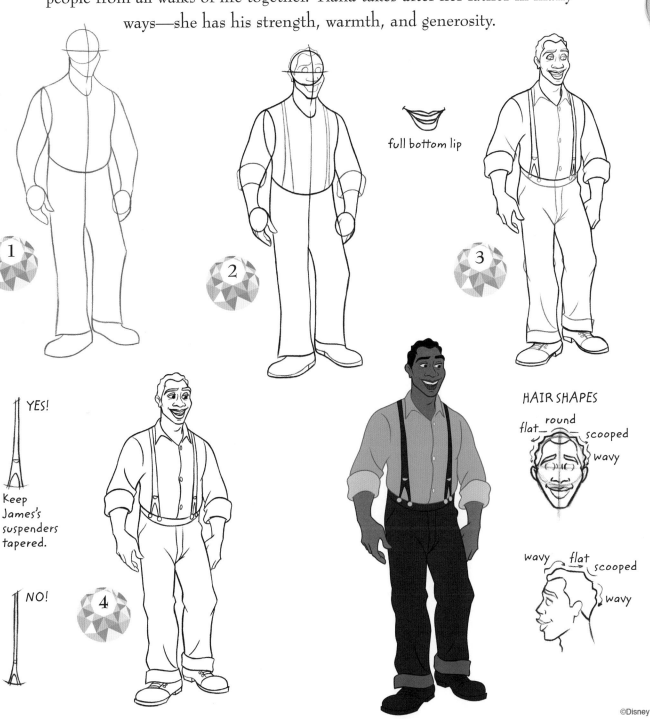

1

2

full bottom lip

3

YES!

Keep James's suspenders tapered.

NO!

4

HAIR SHAPES

flat — round — scooped
wavy

wavy — flat — scooped
wavy

Naveen

Naveen is the handsome, free-spirited, and fun-loving prince from the country of Maldonia. He's a jazz fanatic and has traveled to New Orleans—the birthplace of jazz—to sing, dance, and play to his heart's content. But Naveen's carefree and irresponsible ways have caused his parents to cut him off. Now he's faced with his most dreaded fear: having to work for a living.

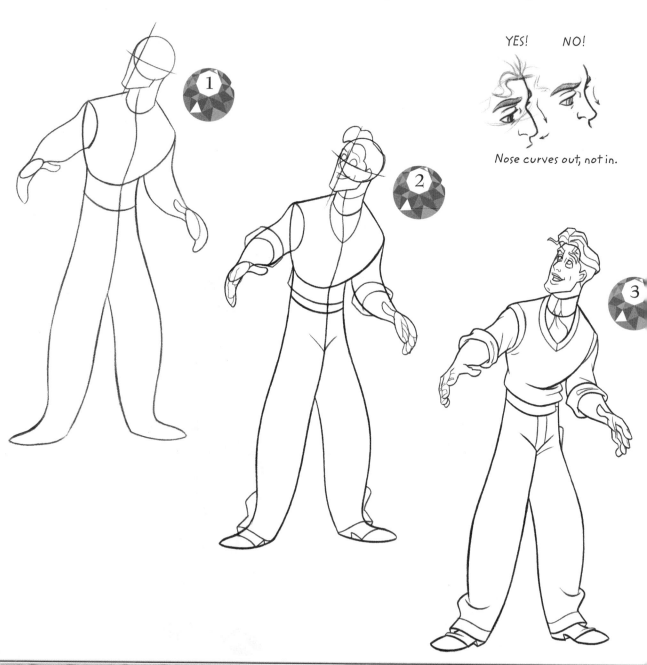

YES!   NO!

Nose curves out, not in.

"For Naveen, everything has to come natural and be a free expression of what he's feeling at that moment. Jazz is the theme of his life."
—Randy Haycock, Disney animator

YES!
Ears are slightly pointed.

NO!
too round

Hands are expressive.

Keep head tall and narrow.

Lawrence

Lawrence is Naveen's stiff, pompous, roly-poly valet. Though he plays the part of the prince's dutiful manservant, Lawrence is secretly envious of the Prince's charm, good looks, and position.

Draw his mouth low on the face.

large lower lip

Lawrence's body is pear-shaped.

Lawrence's nose is round and upturned.

YES!   NO!   NO!

Big Daddy

Big Daddy is Charlotte's father and the wealthiest man in all of Louisiana. Although he is imposing and powerful, he's a big pushover when it comes to Charlotte. Whether it's a new dress for a ball or a prince for a husband, he'll give his daughter anything she wishes for.

1

2

3

Mustache is full and large, ends point up.

S!

NO!

4

Body shape resembles a square.

Charlotte

At eighteen, Charlotte is still a spoiled and self-centered southern belle. She only has one thing on her mind: to marry a prince so she can become a real princess! When Prince Naveen arrives in New Orleans, Charlotte spares no expense to make her dream come true.

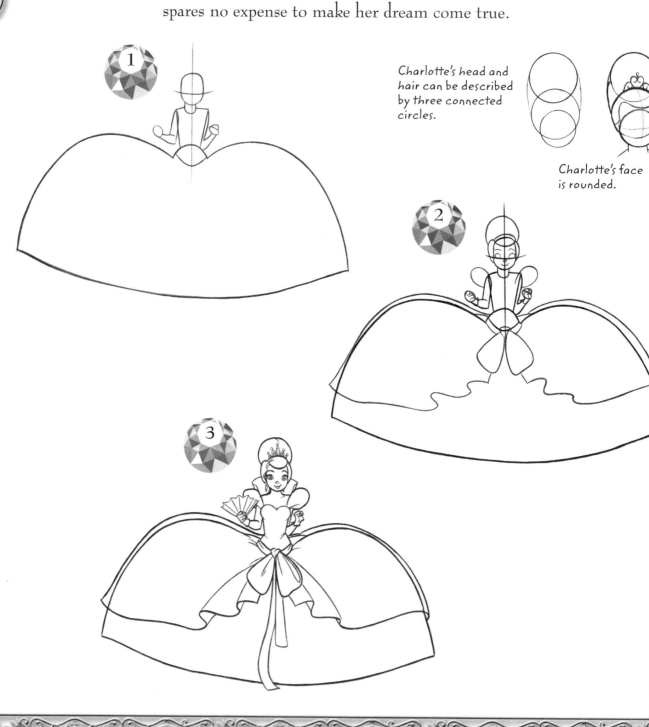

Charlotte's head and hair can be described by three connected circles.

Charlotte's face is rounded.

Eyes are large and round,
but the pupil and iris are small.

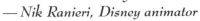 4-5 long lashes

Charlotte uses a fan at
the masquerade ball.

*"Design and exaggeration of the
animation is very important.
Drawing, in some ways, is a means
to an end. Whether I want to convey
a certain performance, or I want a
character to look funny or interesting,
I need to draw to get there."*
— Nik Ranieri, Disney animator

Tiana

Tiana grows up to be an intelligent, beautiful, hardworking young woman, and a very talented cook. She works several waitress jobs and saves every penny. Although her friends often invite her out on the town, she always turns them down. Tiana won't stop working until she has enough money to open the restaurant that she and her father had always dreamed of.

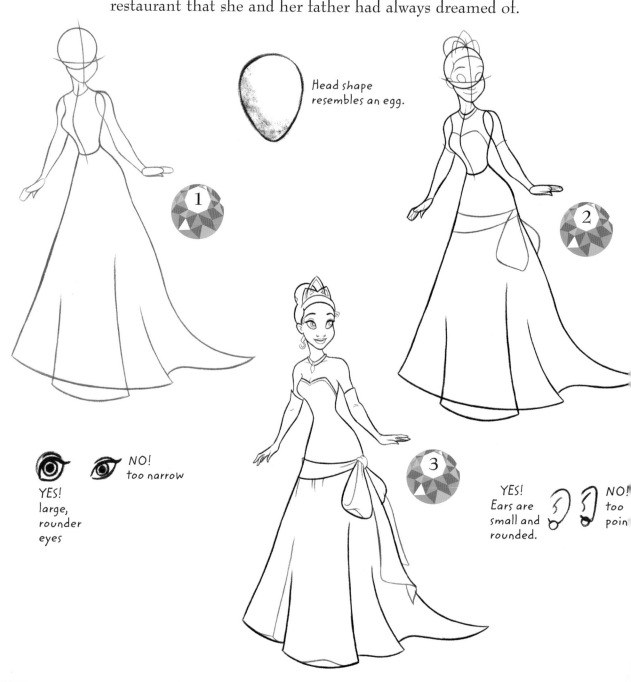

Head shape resembles an egg.

1

2

3

YES! large, rounder eyes

NO! too narrow

YES! Ears are small and rounded.

NO! too poin

"Tiana is the same person throughout. She just literally changes her skin or body. She has similar mannerisms and expressions as a human and as a frog. I never looked at them differently."
—Mark Henn, Disney animator

masquerade ball tiara

Nose is short and round.

rounded chin

Dr. Facilier

Dr. Facilier is a sinister and charismatic man of dark magic who works in the French Quarter. He lures unsuspecting passersby into deals where he promises to give them their heart's desire in return for money. However, when fulfilling those promises, Facilier uses dark magic for his own personal gain. Facilier yearns to expand his small-time business so he can spread darkness and corruption throughout New Orleans…and become fantastically wealthy in the process.

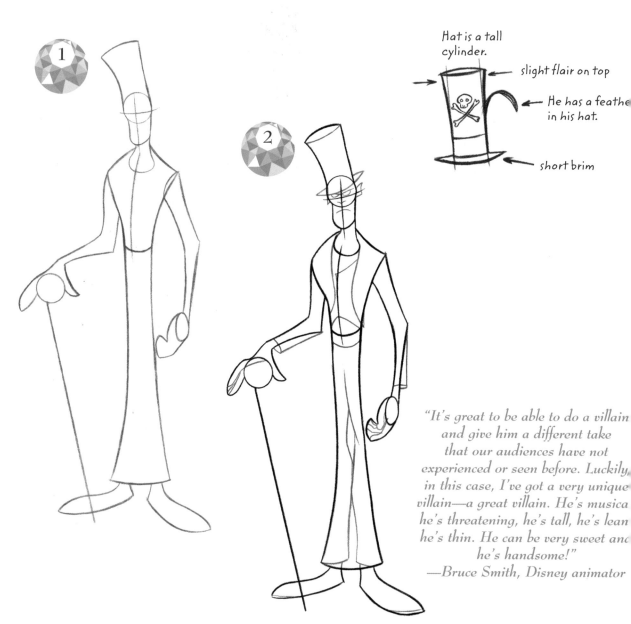

Hat is a tall cylinder.

slight flair on top

He has a feather in his hat.

short brim

"It's great to be able to do a villain and give him a different take that our audiences have not experienced or seen before. Luckily, in this case, I've got a very unique villain—a great villain. He's musical, he's threatening, he's tall, he's lean, he's thin. He can be very sweet and he's handsome!"
—Bruce Smith, Disney animator

3

4

profile

YES!
Ear shape is
more angular.

NO!
too
round

YES! Mustache is
pencil thin.

NO! not too large

Pants are
short, you
can see
his ankles.

Tiana the frog

Being green isn't easy! When Tiana is transformed into a frog, she's faced with brand new challenges: finding her way through the bayou, escaping from frog hunters, and catching flies with her long, sticky tongue! But even as a frog, Tiana proves that she's very capable and hardworking. Whether it's making a boat on which to float down the bayou or whipping up a batch of gumbo for her friends, Tiana can get things done.

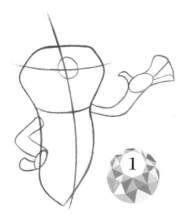

1

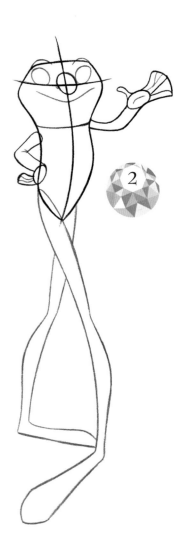

2

Tiana's eyes are one eye's width apart.

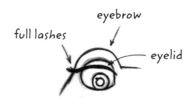

eyebrow

full lashes

eyelid

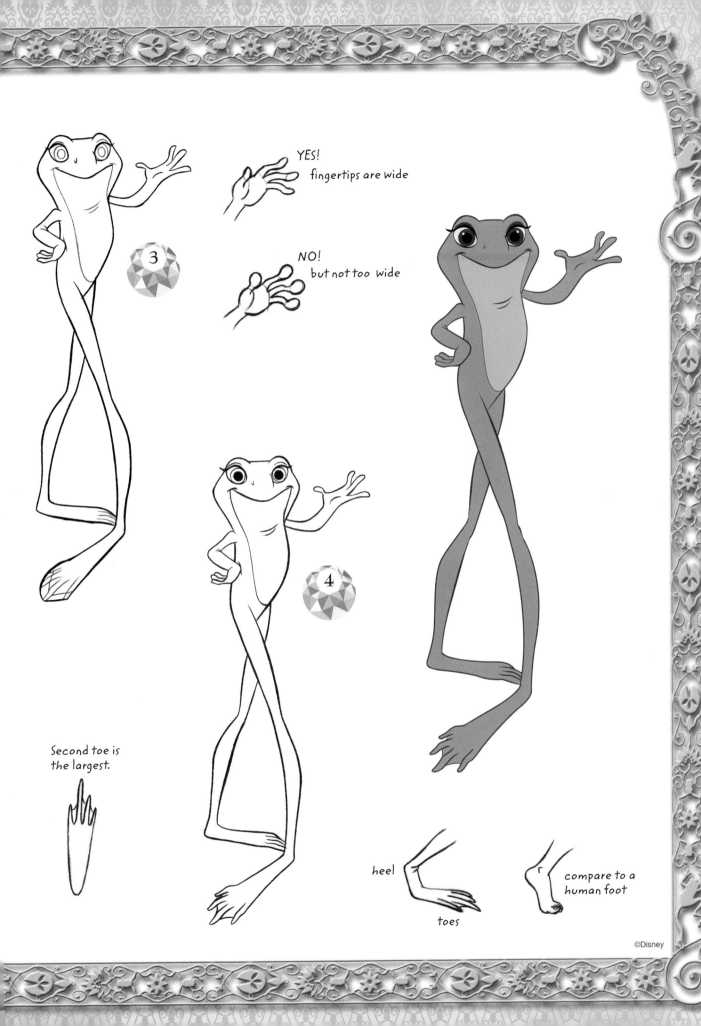

YES!
fingertips are wide

NO!
but not too wide

③

④

Second toe is
the largest.

heel

toes

compare to a
human foot

©Disney

Naveen the frog

When Facilier uses his talisman to cast a spell on Naveen, the prince transforms into a frog. But even in his new amphibious form, Naveen isn't much different. He floats down the bayou river, lounges about, and plays jazz. But when Tiana teaches him a few things about responsibility and hard work, his views begin to change.

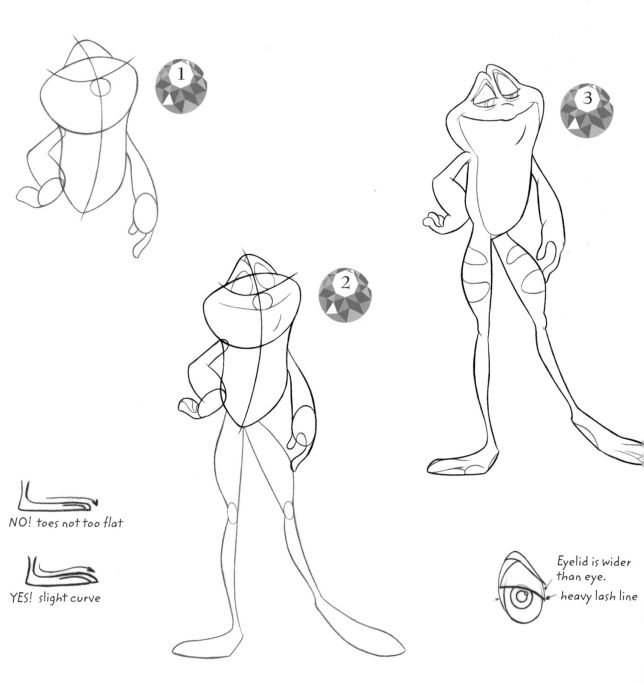

NO! toes not too flat

YES! slight curve

Eyelid is wider than eye.

heavy lash line

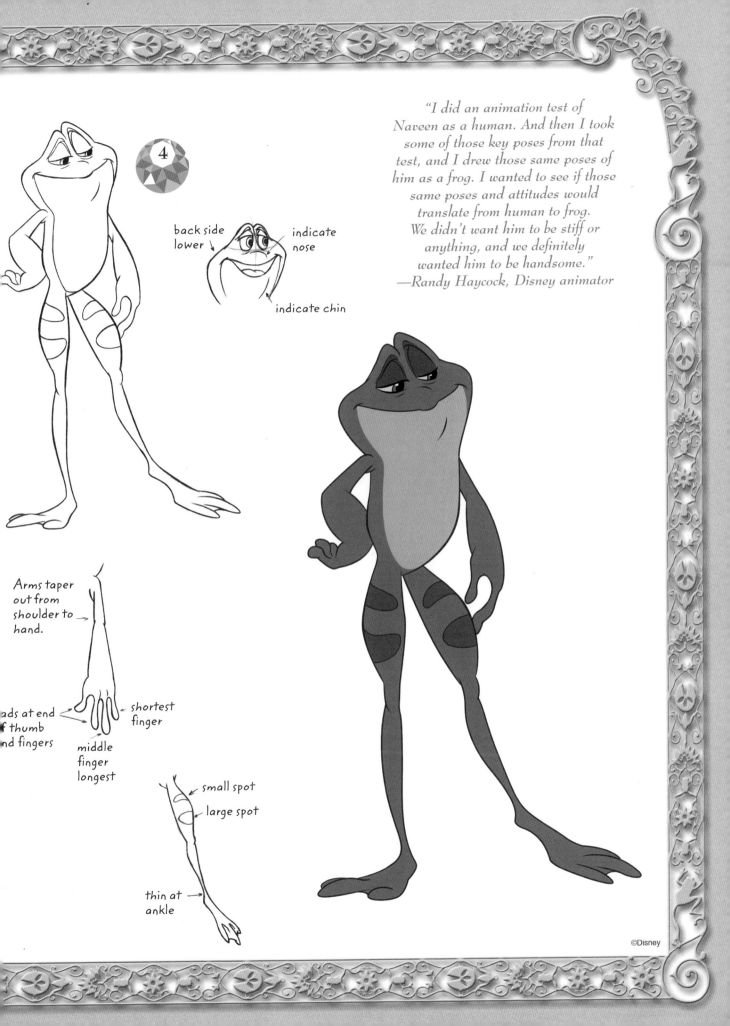

back side lower

indicate nose

indicate chin

"I did an animation test of Naveen as a human. And then I took some of those key poses from that test, and I drew those same poses of him as a frog. I wanted to see if those same poses and attitudes would translate from human to frog. We didn't want him to be stiff or anything, and we definitely wanted him to be handsome."
—Randy Haycock, Disney animator

Arms taper out from shoulder to hand.

...ads at end ...f thumb ...nd fingers

shortest finger

middle finger longest

small spot

large spot

thin at ankle

Louis

Louis is a huge alligator who knows all about jazz, having listened to the great jazz musicians perform on the riverboats passing through the bayou. When he found a discarded trumpet (which he named Giselle), Louis taught himself to play and became a true jazz master himself. His dream is to play for a human audience while not scaring them half to death.

NO!

too round

YES!

Show dimension to eyebrow ridges.

Louis has tiny hands to contrast with his huge body.

Draw this shape first.

Then round out the fingers.

1

2

Muzzle should always have "s-curve" shape.

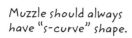

Hanging Louis's jaw way back behind his eyes makes him look like an alligator.

Pupil can protrude off the whites.

"Louis is generally a bundle of nerves in a gator suit...however, Louis has a heart as big as his girth, which he reveals most successfully when blowing his trumpet. Louis's big dream is to play jazz 'with the big boys' in the human world. Now, if it weren't for all those teeth…"
—Eric Goldberg, Disney animator

Ray

Ray is a lovesick Cajun firefly who's constantly pining for his beloved Evangeline—the Evening Star, whom he believes is a firefly. Even though he and Evangeline are from separate worlds, Ray believes love conquers all. Someday they will be together. Ray is also a loyal and courageous friend. He may be small, but he's also mighty! And he's always there to help his friends when they need him.

"When drawing Ray, make sure you have a sense of rhythm. Allow one shape to flow naturally into the next."
—*Mike Surrey, Disney animator*

Don't make chin too round.

YES!

NO!

YES! NO!

antenna shape

3

4

Make wing cutouts asymmetrical.

NO! YES!

Keep legs straighter, with no bend at the knee.

Mama Odie and Juju

Mama Odie is a 200-year-old blind priestess who lives deep in the Louisiana bayou with her "seeing-eye snake," Juju. She's a little forgetful and somewhat scatterbrained but make no mistake: Mama Odie has great powers and is very wise. She befriends Tiana and Naveen and tells them that although they may know what they *want*, they have to discover what they *need*. And only then will they achieve their true dreams.

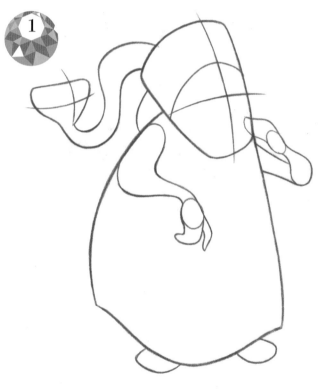

Posture is stooped.

Mama Odie is 2¹/₂ heads tall.

3

YES! Juju's eyes are two ovals, and his pupils are slits.

NO!

4

glasses

YES!   NO!

©Disney

Princess Tiana

When Tiana marries Naveen, she not only regains her human form,
she becomes a princess! Tiana finally gets her dream restaurant
and finds true love with her prince!

Tiana has
dimples on
her cheeks.

Her nose is about
the same width
as the distance
between her eyes.

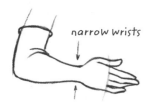

narrow wrists

Tiana's bayou wedding
crown is made of petals
and stamens of varying
shapes and sizes.

3

4

full bottom lip

©Disney

THE PRINCESS AND THE FROG

Now that you've learned the secrets to drawing the characters from *The Princess and the Frog*, try creating scenes from the movie or original scenes of your very own. You can draw Tiana and Naveen as frogs twirling about in the moonlit bayou among their firefly friends; Charlotte in her frilly, pink gown getting ready to meet the prince of her dreams at the masquerade ball; Facilier and his shadows lurking about the French Quarter in search of their next victims; or Louis atop a Mardi Gras float playing his trumpet in a jazz band...the possibilities are endless! To create a little magic of your own, all you need is a piece of paper, a pencil, and your imagination!

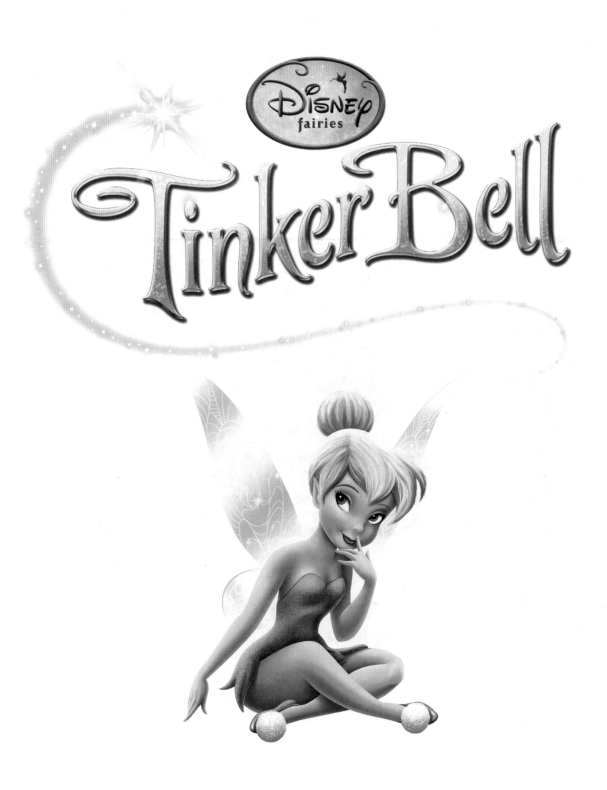

Illustrated by the Disney Storybook Artists

Designed by Shelley Baugh • Project Editor: Rebecca J. Razo

www.disneyfairies.com

Year after year, the seasons come and go—
with a little help from the fairies.

Every fairy starts out as a baby's first laugh, and this story is about one very special laugh. It traveled all the way from wintry London to the magical land of Pixie Hollow. There, the laugh touched down in the Pixie Dust Tree and became a fairy!

All around the new fairy, toadstools sprung up like pedestals. Fairies came forward and placed different objects on the toadstools—a drop of water, a flower, a tiny egg, and more—to help the new arrival find her talent.

The new fairy cautiously approached each object. At first, nothing happened, but when she passed by a small hammer, it began to glow brightly. The fairy queen declared that the new fairy was a tinker—and a very powerful one! Her name was Tinker Bell.

Tinker Bell's first day was a busy one. First she met Clank and Bobble, two other tinkers, and Fairy Mary, the fairy in charge of the workshop in Tinkers' Nook. Later, she helped deliver tools to other fairies. Nature fairies needed the tools to bring spring to the mainland. The mainland was where the big people lived, and Tink thought it sounded wonderful. She couldn't wait to visit!

While Tinker Bell was out making deliveries with her new friends, she met Fawn, Rosetta, Iridessa, and Silvermist. They were nature fairies, and Tink liked them immediately. On the way back to Tinkers' Nook, Tink met Vidia, a fast-flying fairy. Vidia made it clear she didn't think much of the tinkers.

Tink was upset by what Vidia said about tinkers, and she flew away in a huff. As she passed a nearby beach, something caught her eye. She went to take a closer look and discovered many strange objects strewn about the sand. Fascinated, Tinker Bell gathered the objects in her arms and headed home.

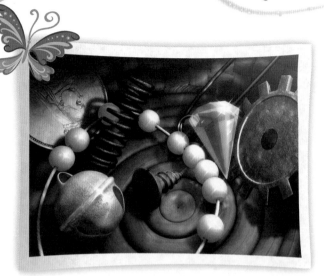

Back at Tinkers' Nook, Tinker Bell showed off her treasures. Fairy Mary said they were junk—Lost Things—washed up from the mainland. She told Tink to get back to work, and Tink reluctantly put the Lost Things away in her workshop.

That night, Queen Clarion was to review the preparations for spring. Tink decided that this was her chance to prove herself, and she rushed to create several devices to make spring preparations easier. But when she tried to demonstrate how to use them, none of them worked. To top off Tink's disappointment, Queen Clarion told her that tinker fairies didn't even go to the mainland! Tinker Bell's efforts had been for nothing. She felt like she didn't matter at all.

But inspiration struck Tinker Bell a second time. She decided she would change her talent! She would become a nature fairy instead of a tinker, and she would go to the mainland after all. Tink tried to be a water fairy, a light fairy, and an animal fairy—but it was no use. Nothing went right and Tink felt worse than ever.

Tinker Bell went to the beach to be alone; there she found a broken music box. By the time her friends caught up with her, she had put it back together—and she'd enjoyed doing it. Tink's friends reminded her that she had a wonderful talent as a tinker. Perhaps this was what she was really meant to do! But tinkers didn't go to the mainland—and Tink still had her heart set on that.

Desperate, Tink asked Vidia for help. The spiteful fairy told Tink that if she could round up the Sprinting Thistles—dangerous weeds that left a path of destruction in their wake—it would prove she was a garden fairy, and then she could go to the mainland! Tink did her best, but the thistles wound up stampeding into Springtime Square. They trampled all the carefully organized springtime supplies, destroying everything.

All the preparations for spring were ruined, and it was Tinker Bell's fault. Tink was about to leave Never Land forever, but she made one last visit to her workshop. She hated to admit it, but she did love to tinker—if only her inventions worked! Looking around her workshop, she had an idea. Tink gathered up the Lost Things she'd found on the beach and spread them out before her. She had work to do.

That night, Tink raced to Springtime Square with her new inventions. She promised everyone that the contraptions she made from the Lost Things could put springtime together again in no time. And she was right! When the sun rose the next morning, the fairies were ready to bring spring to the world. "You did it, Tinker Bell," Queen Clarion said, congratulating her.

Tink was happy—but she was even happier when Fairy Mary told her she could go to the mainland. Her job would be to return the music box she had fixed to its owner! And so, she joined all of her friends as they flew over the sea to the mainland for the change of seasons. Tinker Bell had finally found her place by staying true to herself.

Tools and Materials

The art fairies of Pixie Hollow use tiny, delicate twig-and-feather paintbrushes to paint the spots on ladybugs. But all you'll need for this section are normal, human-sized supplies. To begin, sketch your fairy with a regular pencil. You'll want to have a pencil sharpener and an eraser on hand as well. When you've drawn your fairies just the way you want them, you can bring them to life with a little color! Use crayons, felt-tip markers, watercolors, colored pencils, or even acrylic paints to color in your fairies.

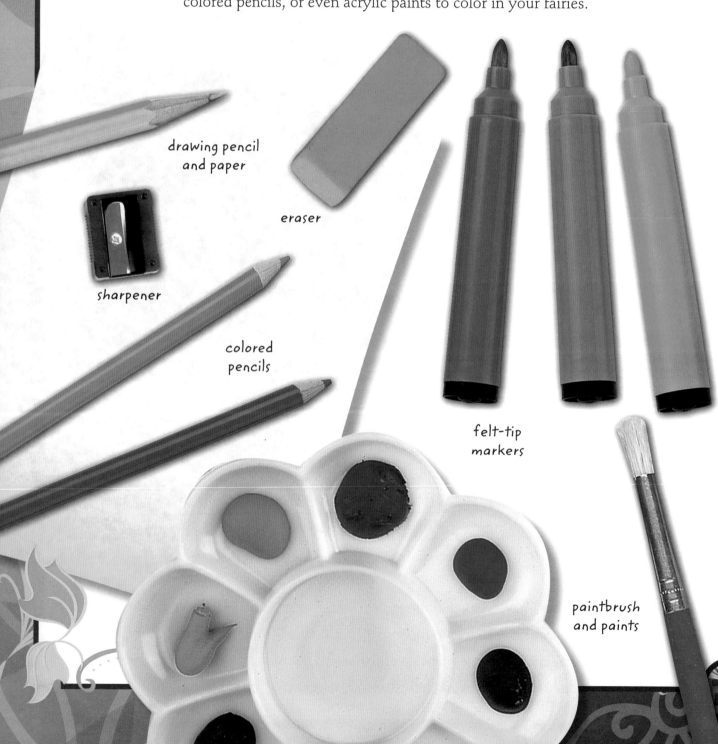

drawing pencil
and paper

eraser

sharpener

colored
pencils

felt-tip
markers

paintbrush
and paints

How to Use This Guide

You don't need the skills of an art fairy to follow these simple steps!

Step 1

First draw the basic shapes using light lines that will be easy to erase.

Step 2

Each new step is shown in blue, so you'll know what to add next.

Step 3

Follow the blue lines to draw the details.

Step 4

Now darken the lines you want to keep and erase the rest.

Step 5

Use fairy magic (or crayons or markers) to add color to your drawing!

Tinker Bell

This spirited tinker fairy is the latest arrival in Pixie Hollow. She shakes things up a bit but soon settles into her new home. Her specialty is inventing contraptions using human objects that wash up on the shores of Never Land. Tink has a big imagination—and an even bigger heart!

Step 1

Step 2

YES!
Bun points up.

NO!
bun not
too low

Tink's hair from
the back

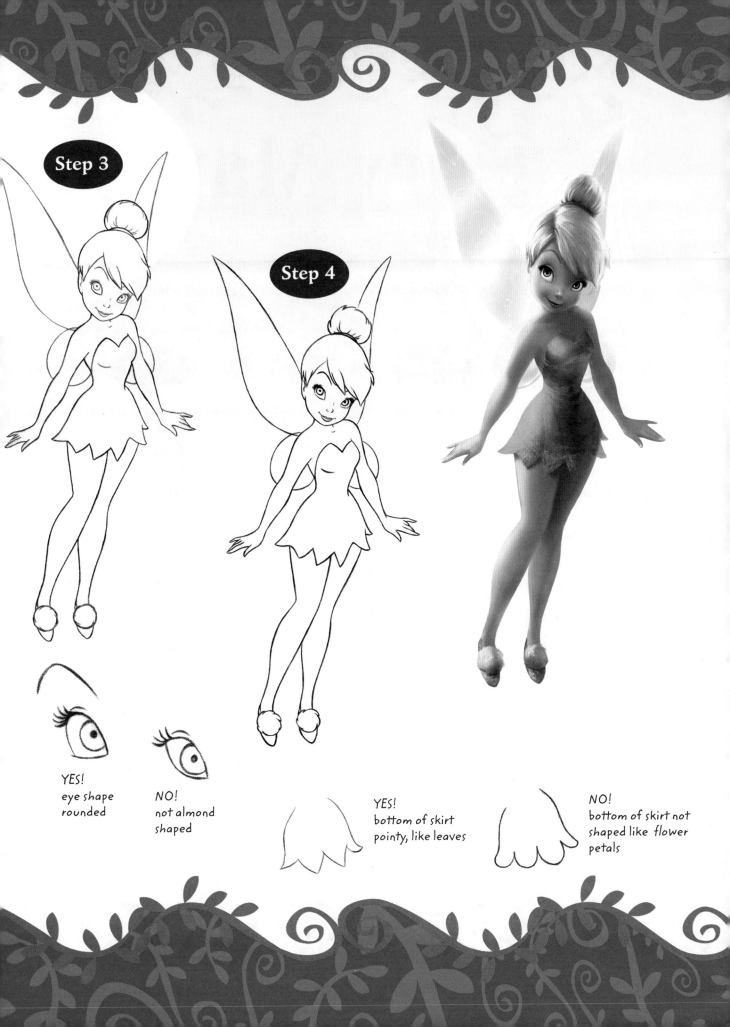

Step 3

Step 4

YES!
eye shape
rounded

NO!
not almond
shaped

YES!
bottom of skirt
pointy, like leaves

NO!
bottom of skirt not
shaped like flower
petals

Fairy Mary

Fairy Mary is the stern, hardworking leader of the tinker fairies. She keeps everything running smoothly in Tinkers' Nook and takes great pride in her talent. She and Tink don't always see eye to eye, but they have great respect for each other.

Think of similarities to these Disney characters:

Nanny,
101 Dalmatians

Merryweather,
Sleeping Beauty

Mrs. Potts,
Beauty and
the Beast

Step 1

Step 2

Step 3

sometimes
carries an
abacus—
a tool for
counting

Step 4

Round shapes
create body
structure.

Silvermist

Friendly and eager to please, the water fairy Silvermist has occasionally been described as "gushy." She's got a good heart, even if she does seem to change her mind every ten minutes!

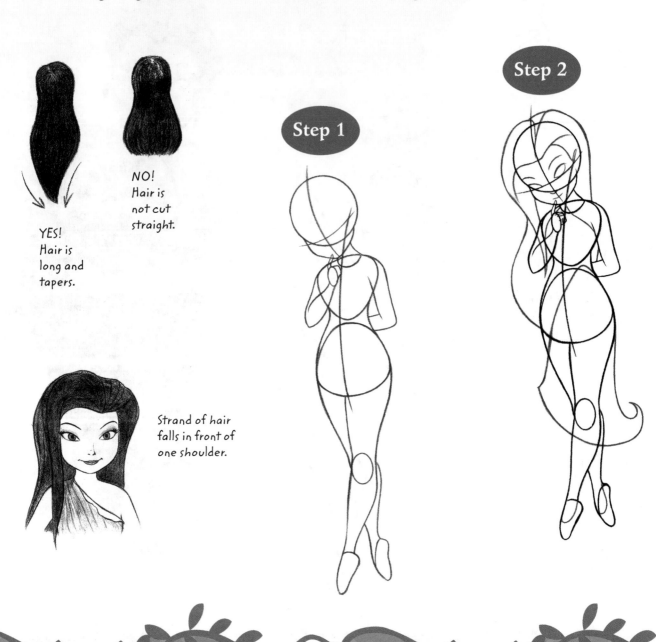

YES!
Hair is
long and
tapers.

NO!
Hair is
not cut
straight.

Strand of hair
falls in front of
one shoulder.

Step 1

Step 2

Step 3

Step 4

Silvermist's dress is made
from lily petals.

YES!
eyes set
at angle

NO!
eyes not
set on
straight
line

Rosetta

Rosetta, a garden fairy, has a quick wit and a ton of charm.
Beautiful and sensible, Rosetta sees right to the heart of every problem.

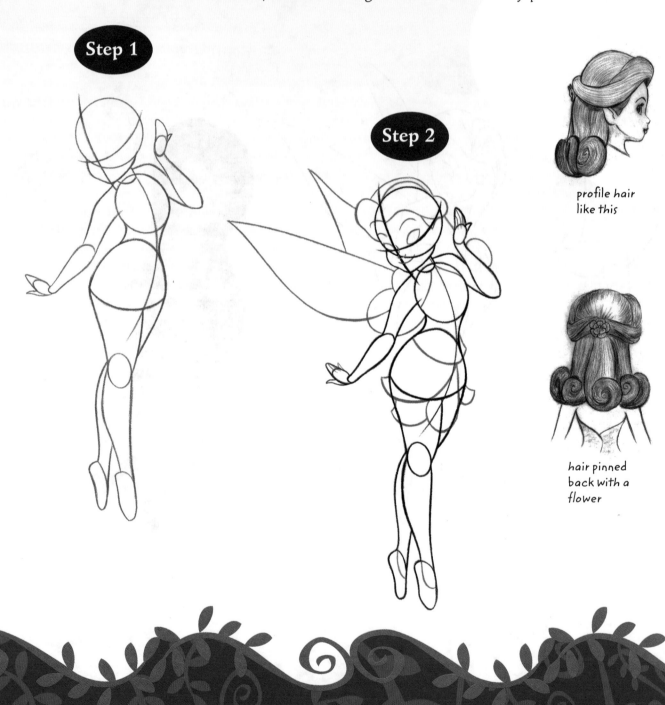

Step 1

Step 2

profile hair
like this

hair pinned
back with a
flower

Step 3

Step 4

YES!

NO!

Rosetta's dress is made from rose petals.

Iridessa

Iridessa is a thoughtful fairy who likes to do everything exactly right, especially when it comes to he job. No other light fairy catches the last rays of sunlight with quite the same precision as Iridessa.

Step 1

Step 2

YES!
slender chin,
full lips

NO!
cheeks not
too full

YES!
hair in
sections

NO!
hair not
smooth

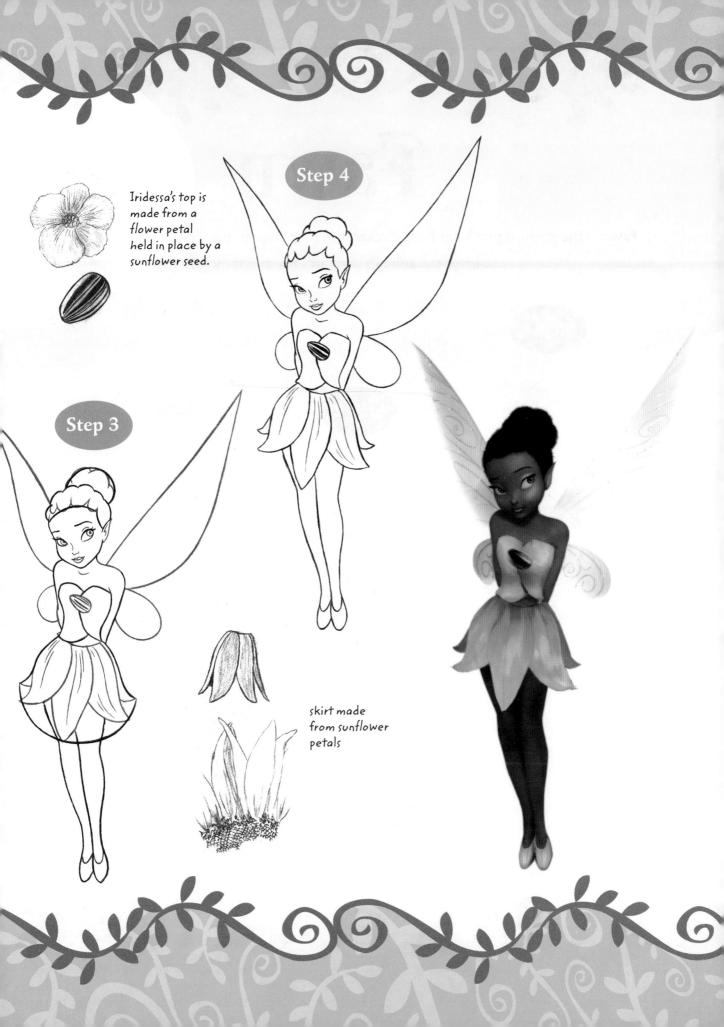

Iridessa's top is
made from a
flower petal
held in place by a
sunflower seed.

Step 4

Step 3

skirt made
from sunflower
petals

Fawn

Fawn is the greatest prankster Pixie Hollow has ever known, but she's also the biggest softie. She loves the animals she cares for, and they love her.

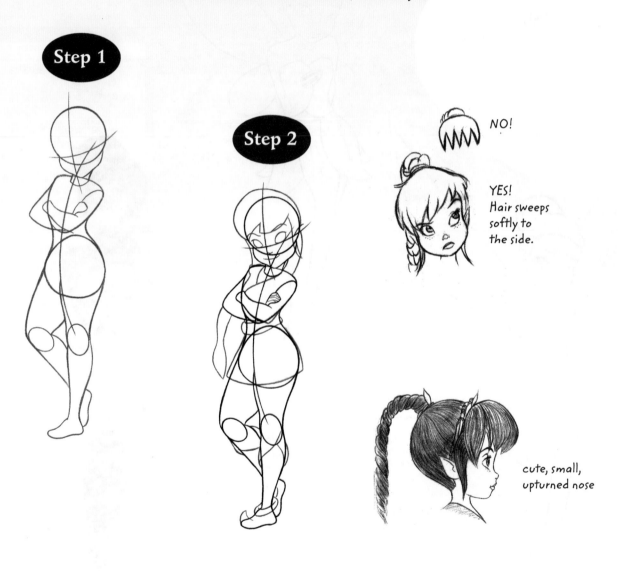

Step 1

Step 2

NO!

YES!
Hair sweeps
softly to
the side.

cute, small,
upturned nose

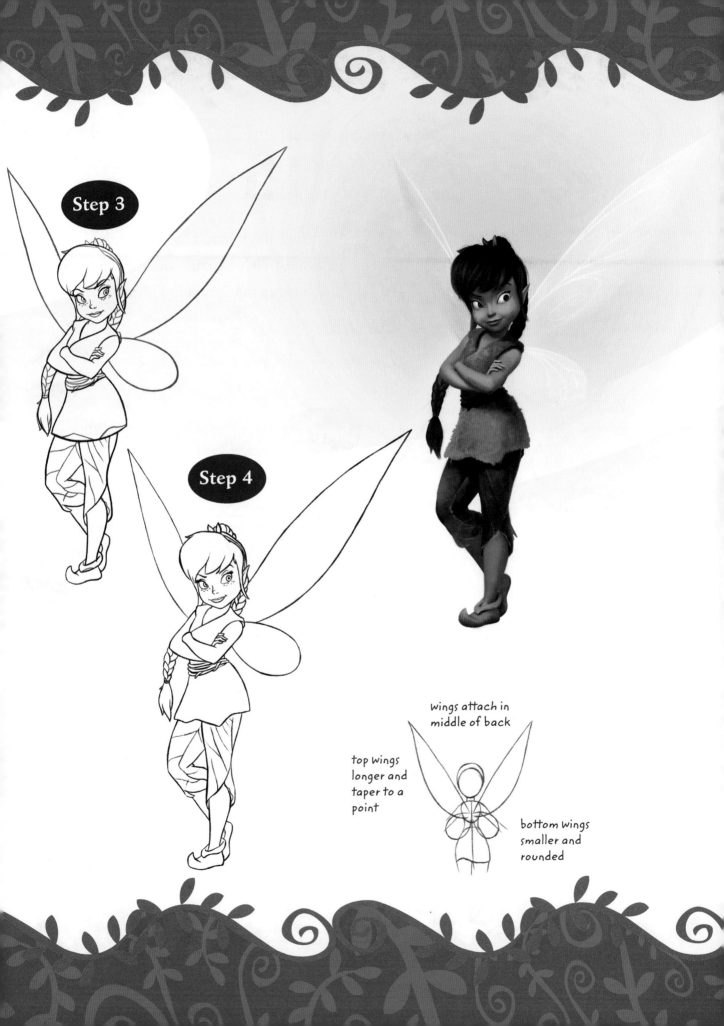

Step 3

Step 4

wings attach in
middle of back

top wings
longer and
taper to a
point

bottom wings
smaller and
rounded

Vidia

Spiteful Vidia loves being known for her talent and resents any competition—especially from Tinker Bell. But Vidia's schemes against Tink backfire, and the fast-flying fairy is left with the thankless job of rounding up the Sprinting Thistles.

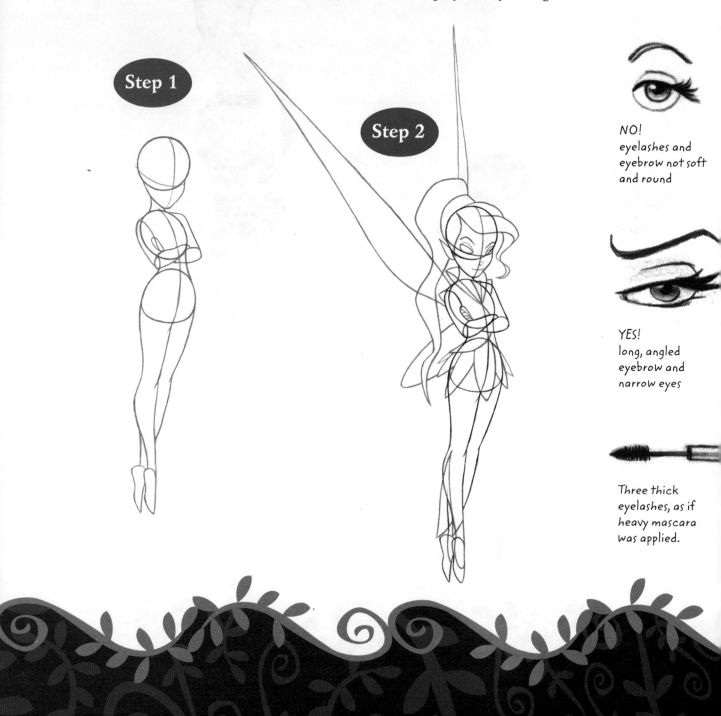

Step 1

Step 2

NO!
eyelashes and eyebrow not soft and round

YES!
long, angled eyebrow and narrow eyes

Three thick eyelashes, as if heavy mascara was applied.

Step 3

Step 4

YES!
Ponytail twists
and turns.

NO!
ponytail not
straight

Queen Clarion

Queen Clarion is the wise ruler of the fairies. Her magic is so powerful that she sometimes travels in a mist of pure pixie dust.

Queen Clarion wears thr
different crowns dependi
on the occasion:

everyday crown

arrival crown

spring crown

Step 1

Step 2

Step 4

Queen Clarion's wings are like a butterfly's.

Step 3

YES!
Eyes are almond shaped.

NO!
not too round

Clank

Clank and Bobble are the very best of friends. There's no trouble these two tinkers haven't gotten into! They really admire Tinker Bell for her talent and skill.

Step 1

Step 2

Clank puts cotton in his ears when he's working.

Step 3

Clank is shaped like a fig.

Step 4

He wears a tunic made from a leaf.

He carries a jug made from a nutshell.

Bobble

Bobble likes to hang out with his good friend Clank. These goofy pals love to fiddle, fix, craft, and create. Bobble's "glasses" are actually dewdrops set in blades of grass!

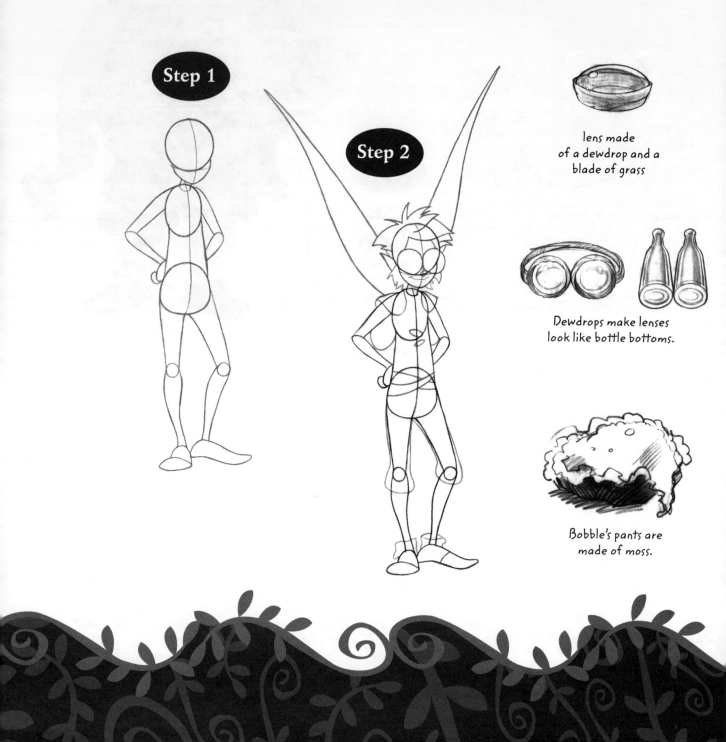

Step 1

Step 2

lens made of a dewdrop and a blade of grass

Dewdrops make lenses look like bottle bottoms.

Bobble's pants are made of moss.

Step 3

Bobble is thin—like a twig.

Step 4

YES!
hair thick and wavy on top; short in back

NO!
hair not flat and long

Terence

Terence is a dust-keeper fairy and Tinker Bell's best friend. He knows how important each and every fairy talent is and takes great pride in the work he does for the fairies of Pixie Hollow.

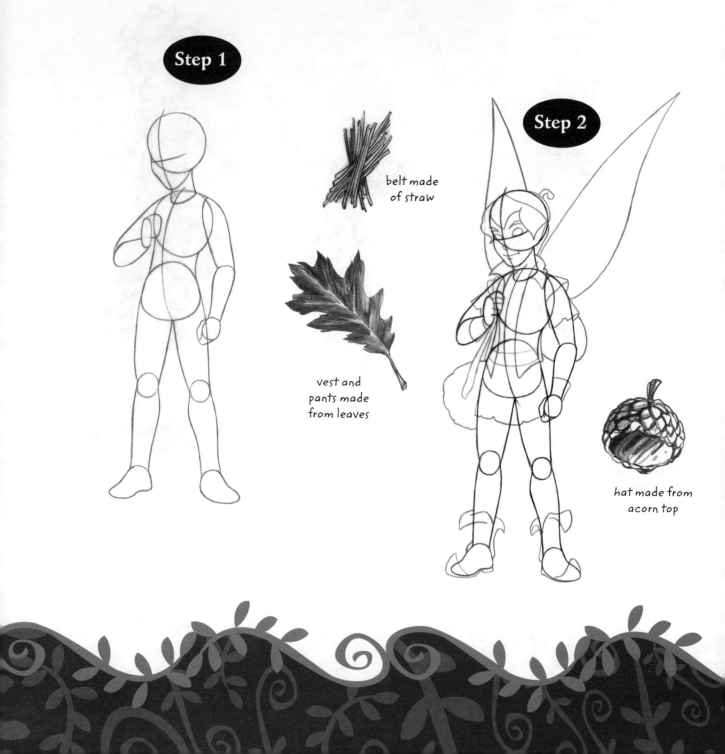

Step 1

Step 2

belt made
of straw

vest and
pants made
from leaves

hat made from
acorn top

Step 3

dispenses daily
rations of pixie dust

Step 4

shoulder bag
made from
walnut shell

Draw Your Own Fairy Scene

In enchanted Pixie Hollow, where the fairies of Never Land live, all four seasons exist at once. The snowflake fairies practice their arts in Winter Woods, while the fairies of Summer Glade sweeten peaches with pixie dust. And nearby, autumn and spring fairies are always busy as well. Tinker Bell's favorite view of Never Land is from high up in the air, where she can see every corner of her magical home.

Here's your chance to draw a scene from Pixie Hollow! First sketch an outline of your scene. Then add animals, plants, flowers, trees, or other fairy friends. Add color with crayons or markers. Be creative and have fun!

In Pixie Hollow, every day is full of magic.

MICKEY MOUSE

Illustrated and Designed by
John Loter and the
Disney Publishing
Creative Development Staff

WELCOME

Hi! It's your old pal Mickey!

Do you like to draw? I sure do! It's a lot of fun! This guide will help you become an even better artist than you are now!

I've opened my sketchbook with all the secret information—how tall Goofy is . . . how to draw Minnie's shoes. . . . It's easy when you know how! The whole gang is going to help you out along the way. I'll meet you at the end of the section!

MICKEY

THE GANG

Before we get started, let's get to know Mickey and his friends.

MICKEY MOUSE

Mickey Mouse is always friendly and outgoing. Everybody likes him.

MINNIE MOUSE

Minnie Mouse is Mickey Mouse's sweetheart and friend.

DONALD DUCK

Donald Duck has quite a temper, but he's still lots of fun to be around.

Check out how big (or small) the characters are compared to one another. When you draw them together, you'll want to make sure you don't make Donald taller than Goofy! Remember that everyone is just about the same height except Goofy, who's the tallest.

DAISY DUCK

GOOFY

PLUTO

Daisy Duck is Donald's favorite gal. She's quite fashionable.

Goofy is a pretty silly guy. Make sure you draw him having lots of fun.

Pluto's one happy pup! His best pal is Mickey Mouse, who also happens to be his owner.

BASICS

Before learning to draw the characters, it's a good idea to get warmed up. Start by drawing simple shapes like circles and ovals. Don't worry about making them perfect; just keep your wrist nice and loose. When you feel comfortable with your shapes, move on to the steps.

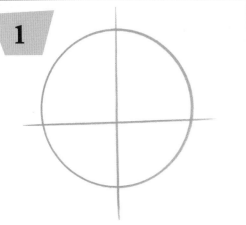

1

The first thing you'll draw are guidelines to help position the features of the character.

Usually artists draw characters in several steps. Sometimes the steps are different, depending on what you're drawing. The important thing to remember is to start simply and add details later. The blue lines show each new step, and the black lines show what you've already drawn.

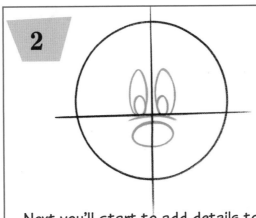

2

Next you'll start to add details to your drawing. It will take several steps to add all the details.

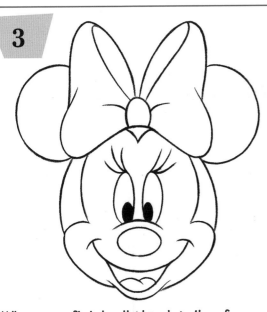

3

When you finish all the details of your drawing, you can go back and erase the guidelines. You can also darken your lines with a pen or marker.

Goofy's learned all the steps, and now he's ready to paint the finished drawing!

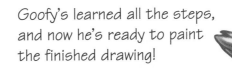

MICKEY MOUSE

Drawing Mickey's Face

STEP 1

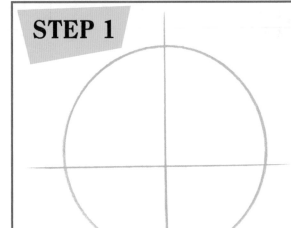

Start with a circle. Add center lines to help position Mickey's features.

STEP 2

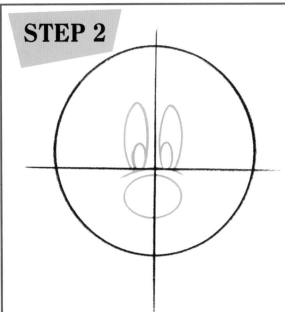

Now add Mickey's eyes and nose. His eyes rest on the edge of one center line. Add a little curve right below his eyes.

STEP 3

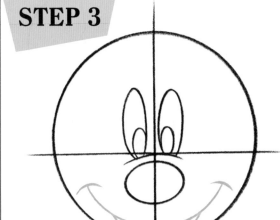

Add Mickey's smile and chin. The top portion of his mouth follows the same curve as his nose. See how his chin extends below the circle of his head.

Pluto is Mickey's favorite pu
and Mickey is Pluto's best p

STEP 4

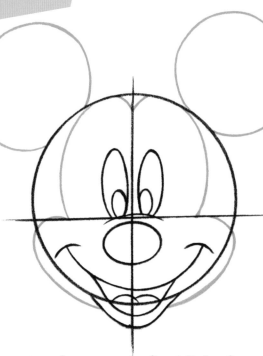

Draw two large ovals for Mickey's ears. Add curved lines to form the area around his cheeks and eyes. (This is called the "mask.")

STEP 5

Erase your guidelines and clean up the drawing.

STEP 6

Now color your drawing of Mickey.

BE SURE TO MAKE HIM HANDSOME!

MICKEY MOUSE

Drawing Mickey's Body

When drawing the characters' bodies, notice the curved line going from top to bottom in Step 1. This line is called the **line of action.** The line of action is a guideline to give your character direction and movement.

STEP 1

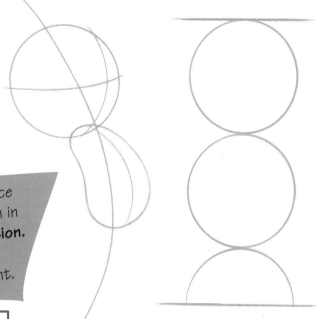

Start with a circle. Add a pear shape for Mickey's body. Mickey's height is 2½ times the size of his head.

STEP 2

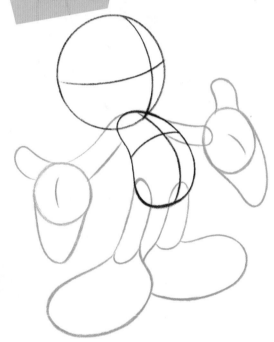

Add Mickey's arms, legs, hands, and feet.

When the tops of Mickey's hands show, be sure to add the stitching lines to his gloves!

STEP 3

Add Mickey's ears, pants, and shoes!

STEP 4

Fill in all the details for Mickey's face that you learned on the previous pages. Don't forget to add his tail!

STEP 5

Erase your guidelines and clean up the drawing.

Mickey's shoes are slightly longer than his hands.

STEP 6

Now color your drawing of Mickey.

MINNIE MOUSE
Drawing Minnie's Face

STEP 1

Start with a circle. Add center lines to help position Minnie's features, just as you did for Mickey.

STEP 2

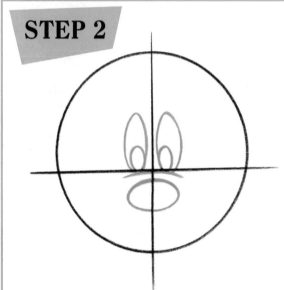

Add Minnie's eyes and nose. Her eyes rest on the edge of one center line.

STEP 3

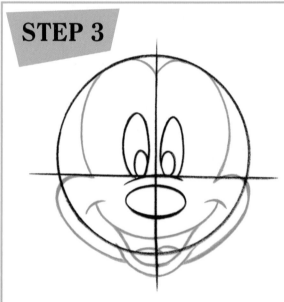

Add Minnie's smile and chin. The top portion of her mouth follows the same curve as her nose. See how her chin extends below the circle of her head. Add curved lines to form the mask.

Minnie and Daisy are the very best of friends.

STEP 4

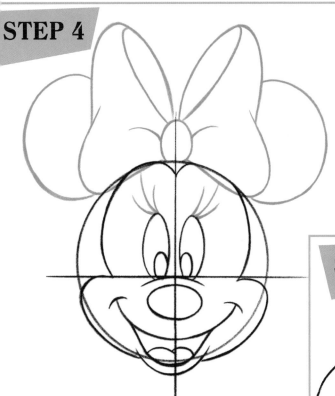

Draw two large ovals for Minnie's ears and a great big bow on top of her head. Don't forget her eyelashes!

Minnie's eyelashes: the middle lashes are longer than the others.

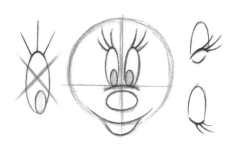

STEP 5

Erase your guidelines and clean up the drawing.

STEP 6

Now color your drawing of Minnie.

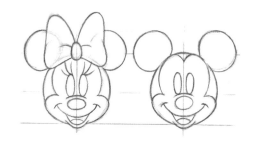

Minnie's and Mickey's heads are similar, but Minnie's eyes are slightly larger and wider than Mickey's. Her open mouth is slightly smaller than his.

MINNIE MOUSE
Drawing Minnie's Body

STEP 1

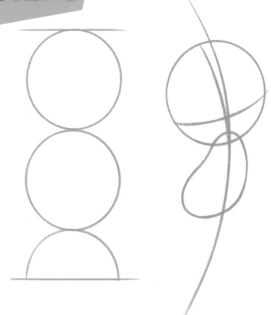

Start with a circle. Add a bean shape for Minnie's body. Minnie's height is 2½ times the size of her head.

STEP 2

Add Minnie's arms, legs, hands, and feet.

Minnie's shoes have a wide, rounded toe and thick, high heels.

STEP 3

Add Minnie's ears, dress, bow, and shoes.

STEP 4

Fill in all the details for Minnie's face that you learned on the previous pages. Don't forget to add her tail!

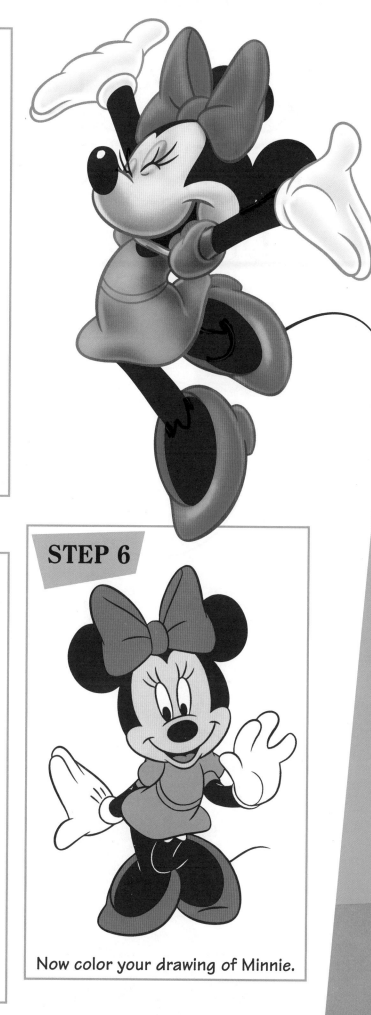

STEP 5

Erase your guidelines and clean up the drawing.

STEP 6

Now color your drawing of Minnie.

DONALD DUCK

Drawing Donald's Face

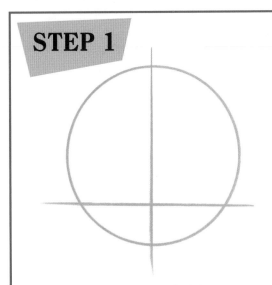

Start with a circle. Add center lines to help position the features

STEP 2

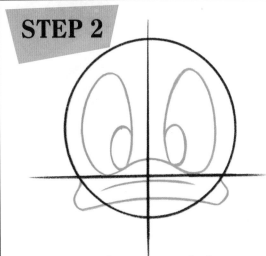

Add Donald's eyes and the top of his bill. His eyes rest on the edge of one center line. Draw the curved lines for his bill.

STEP 3

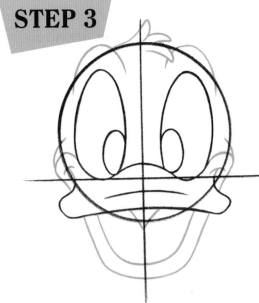

Add Donald's eyebrows and tufts on the top of his head. See how his lower bill curves below his head. His cheeks are very curvy when he smiles. Now add a little triangle for his tongue.

Goofy's silly attitude sometimes irritat the hot-tempered Donald, but Mickey usually manages to keep the peace.

STEP 4

Add Donald's cap. See how the hatband and the ribbon are the same width.

STEP 5

Erase your guidelines and clean up the drawing.

...onald's hat is ...ft and flexible ...t always holds ...s shape.

STEP 6

Now color your drawing of Donald.

GAWRSH! THAT'S A FUNNY HAT!

DONALD DUCK
Drawing Donald's Body

STEP 1

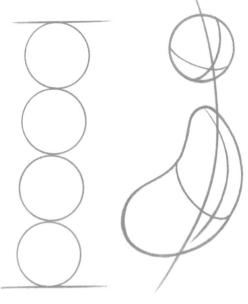

Start with a circle. Add a jelly bean shape for Donald's body. Donald's height is about 4 times the size of his head.

STEP 2

Add Donald's arms, legs, hands, feet, and bill.

Donald's hands are almost as long as the height of his head.

STEP 3

Sketch in Donald's clothes.

STEP 4

Draw Donald's features as you learned on the previous pages. Add the details of his clothes. Don't forget his tail!

STEP 5

Erase your guidelines and clean up the drawing.

STEP 6

Now color your drawing of Donald.

DAISY DUCK

Drawing Daisy's Face

Start with a circle. Add cross lines to help position Daisy's features.

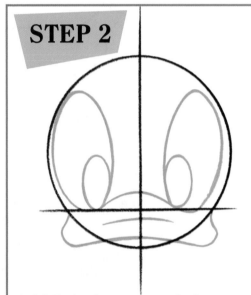

Add Daisy's eyes and the top of her bill. Notice how her eyes are rounder and more angled than Donald's. The bottoms of her eyes and the top of her bill fit together smoothly.

Add Daisy's eyebrows and the lower part of her bill. Now add the little triangle for her tongu just as you did for Donald.

Daisy is just crazy about Dona

STEP 4

Add Daisy's bow and eyelashes. She has three eyelashes over each eye. The middle lashes are longer than the others.

STEP 5

Erase your guidelines and clean up the drawing.

STEP 6

Now color your drawing of Daisy.

BETTER SHARPEN YOUR PENCIL FOR DAISY'S EYELASHES!

DAISY DUCK
Drawing Daisy's Body

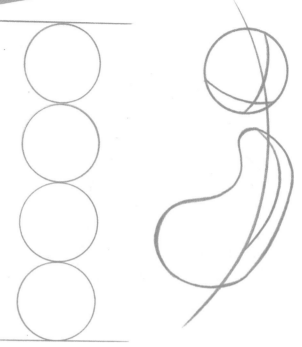

STEP 1

Start with a circle. Add a curved pear shape for Daisy's body. Daisy's height is about 4 times the size of her head.

STEP 2

Add Daisy's arms, legs, hands, feet, and bill.

Daisy's bracelet hangs loosely from her left wrist.

STEP 3

Sketch in Daisy's clothes. Don't forget her bracelet.

STEP 4

Fill in all the details of Daisy's head and clothes. Add a small tuft of feathers for her tail.

STEP 5

Erase your guidelines and clean up the drawing.

STEP 6

Now color your drawing of Daisy.

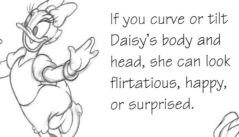

If you curve or tilt Daisy's body and head, she can look flirtatious, happy, or surprised.

GOOFY
Drawing Goofy's Face

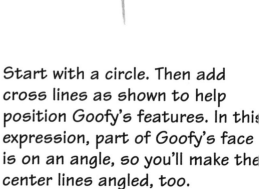

Start with a circle. Then add cross lines as shown to help position Goofy's features. In this expression, part of Goofy's face is on an angle, so you'll make the center lines angled, too.

STEP 2

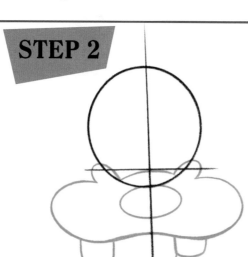

Add a squished oval beneath the circle for Goofy's nose. Then add his cheeks, teeth, and mouth.

STEP 3

Add Goofy's big oval eyes and tongue.

Goofy's head is similar to Pluto's.

STEP 4

Add Goofy's hat and ears. His ears are like big teardrops.

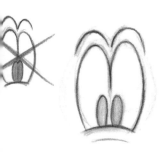

Notice how the whites of Goofy's eyes touch each other. Just make sure you keep his pupils separate.

STEP 5

Erase your guidelines and clean up the drawing.

STEP 6

Now color your drawing of Goofy.

Goofy's hat is about 1 head long. It's squishy looking and leans to one side.

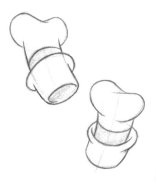

GOOFY
Drawing Goofy's Body

STEP 1

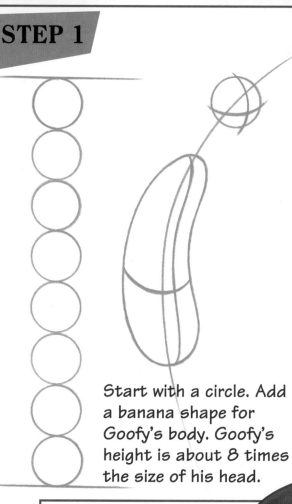

Start with a circle. Add a banana shape for Goofy's body. Goofy's height is about 8 times the size of his head.

STEP 2

Sketch in Goofy's arms, legs, hands, feet, and head.

Goofy has BIG feet.

The toes of his shoes turn up slightly.

STEP 3

Add Goofy's clothes.

STEP 4

Fill in the details of Goofy's face and clothes.

STEP 5

Erase your guidelines and clean up the drawing.

Use Goofy's entire body to act out a mood or action.

STEP 6

Now color your drawing of Goofy.

Goofy's loose-limbed body is capable of a wide variety of poses.

PLUTO
Drawing Pluto's Body

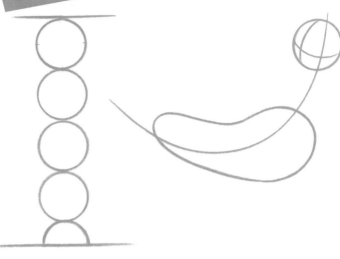

STEP 1

Start with a circle. Add a pear shape for Pluto's body. Pluto's height is about 4½ times the size of his head.

STEP 2

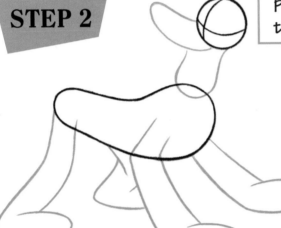

Sketch in Pluto's legs and head.

STEP 3

Start to add Pluto's face and ears. Sketch in his collar and add some detail to his feet for his toes.

Pluto has three pads on the bottom of each paw.

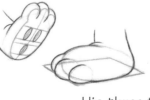

His three toes are stubby.

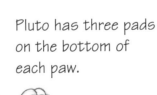

STEP 4

Fill in all the details for Pluto's head. Don't forget to add his tail.

Pluto's ears can act together to accentuate a mood or an expressive pose.

STEP 5

Erase your guidelines and clean up the drawing.

His collar hangs loosely at the back of his neck.

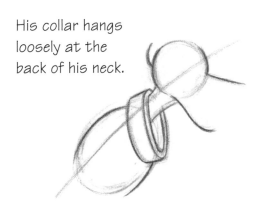

STEP 6

Now color your drawing of Pluto.

COLORING STYLES

You can color your drawings in many different ways.

Some artists like pastels.

Be careful! You don't want to make a mess the way Goofy does.

ur final picture
l look different
pending on how
u choose to
or it.

You can always
use crayons or
colored pencils.
Then maybe add
some paint.

Watercolors and
tempera paints can
be fun, too!

GOOD LUCK

boys and girls!

Now that you've learned how to draw your favorite characters, try experimenting on your own. Remember to use your imagination—and have fun!

THE LITTLE MERMAID

Illustrated by
Philo Barnhart
Diana Wakeman

Designed by Joshua Morris Publishing, Inc.

The Making of *The Little Mermaid*

After the overwhelming success of *Snow White and the Seven Dwarfs,* Walt Disney immediately began work on a number of new projects, one of which was *The Little Mermaid.*

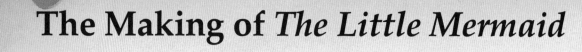

This moving story of courage and love seemed a natural for animation. Preliminary story sketches were made, but work was halted with the outbreak of World War II. It wasn't until 1986 that the Disney Studios again turned its attention to the plight of Hans Christian Andersen's little mermaid.

The Little Mermaid featured more underwater action than any previous Disney film. The artists soon learned that the movement, weight, and speed of the characters were directly influenced by their watery environment. Hundreds of iridescent bubbles, gently waving seaweed, and brilliant tropical

fish made King Triton's kingdom the most fabulous ever designed. Authentic details on Prince Eric's ship and a magnificent castle by the sea show the care taken to ensure that *The Little Mermaid* would become another animation classic.

The huge success of *The Little Mermaid* is largely due to the careful development of each of its characters. From Ariel's pert chin to Sebastian's drooping eyelids, no detail was overlooked.

Ariel's character was developed by studying a wide variety of human and cartoon models.

In order to get an idea of what Ariel should look like, Disney artists scoured hundreds of magazines looking for a face that was fresh, young, and appealing. There were discussions about whether Ariel should be glamorous and exotic or cute and athletic. Part of the research included a review of past Disney heroines. Ariel is most similar to Alice (from *Alice in Wonderland*) in appearance. Both have a large forehead, long, loose hair, wide-set eyes, and a small mouth and chin.

The non-human characters gave the artists an even broader range of ideas with which to work. The character of Ursula the Sea Witch was originally designed as a mermaid. She was then given an eel's tail. But after

Alice

Ariel

Even in the earliest sketches, Ursula's wicked nature was apparent.

viewing a film of an octopus moving across the ocean floor, the Disney artists knew they had found the right way to express Ursula's extravagant personality. As for Sebastian, his deep voice and melodramatic statements seemed all the more humorous coming from a tiny crab. And Scuttle the seagull's dark eyebrows and expressive round eyes were based closely on those of the man who gave him voice, Buddy Hackett.

Drawing Techniques

Drawing Ariel and her friends can be fun and rewarding. With a little patience and practice, you will soon be producing successful drawings of your own.

Most characters are based on simple round and oval shapes. Using a light, continuous motion, sketch around and around until you've made a circle or oval that is the correct shape. Also practice drawing curves with smooth strokes. You may then erase any stray lines for a clean look. Try sketching a variety of sizes, or join shapes together to create new shapes.

Most Disney characters are drawn with a ball for the head and a line of action showing the direction of the body. This line gives your character movement and life. It should flow naturally and smoothly.

It's useful to transfer the outline of your drawing onto tracing paper. This gives you a silhouette that reflects the character's proportions and shows if you have created a clear, strong pose. A good silhouette leads to a good finished drawing.

Once you've drawn your character, carefully erase the line of action and other construction lines to clean up your drawing. Now you're ready to color Ariel.

Ariel's Head

The three-quarter view is the best angle to use to make a character look three-dimensional. Notice how much depth, form, and structure can be achieved in this drawing.

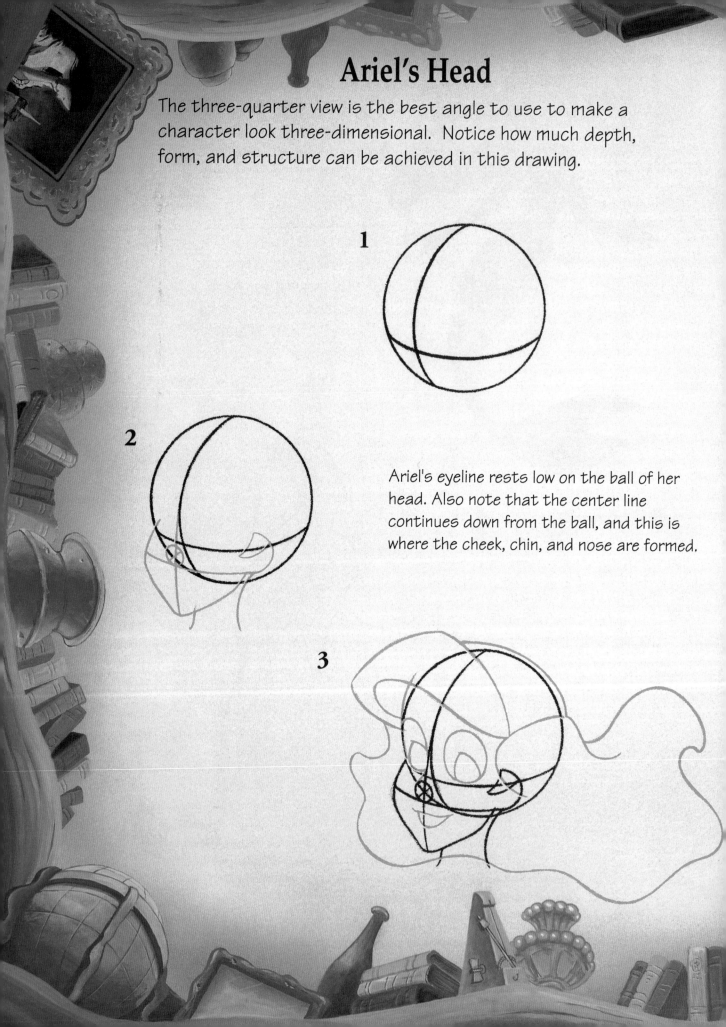

1

2

Ariel's eyeline rests low on the ball of her head. Also note that the center line continues down from the ball, and this is where the cheek, chin, and nose are formed.

3

5

6

Ariel's Expressions

Knowing the attitude you would like to portray can make the character more believable. Even though expressions create shape changes in Ariel's face, the head volume remains the same.

determined

daydreaming

enchanted

happy

surprised

concerned

amused

Ariel Three-Quarter View

People around the world have been charmed by Ariel's cheerful enthusiasm. Be sure to show some of her energy when drawing her complete figure.

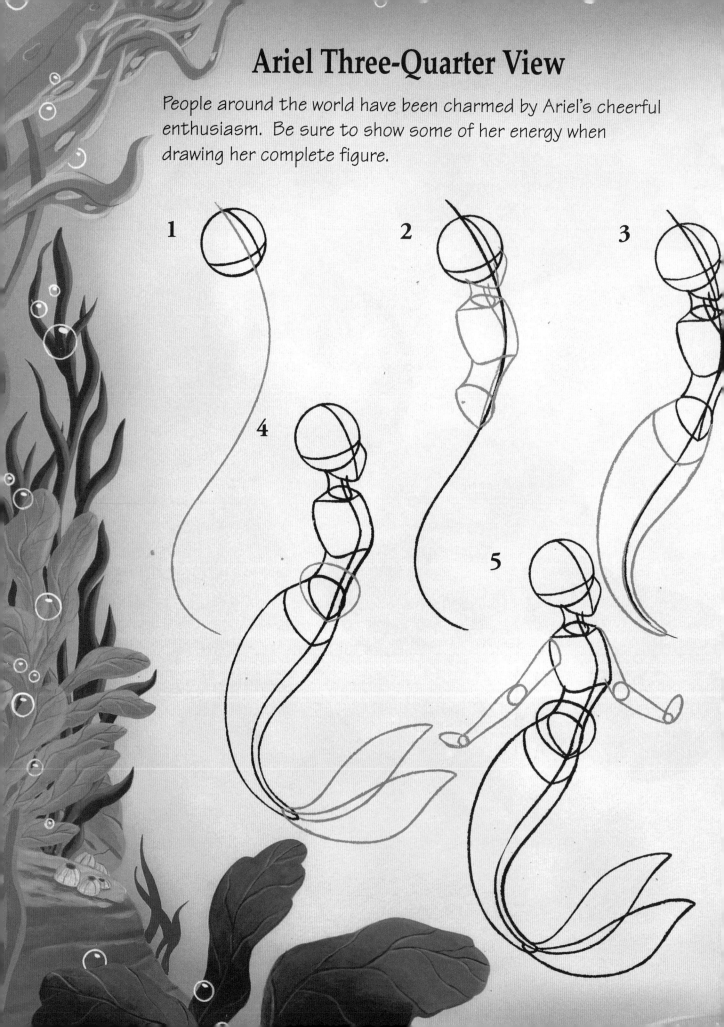

6

7

8

A strong line of action will help give the feeling that Ariel's body flows naturally into her graceful tail.

Sebastian

Sebastian is a little crab with a big voice and a big heart, as well. Try to bring out the warmer side of his personality when drawing him.

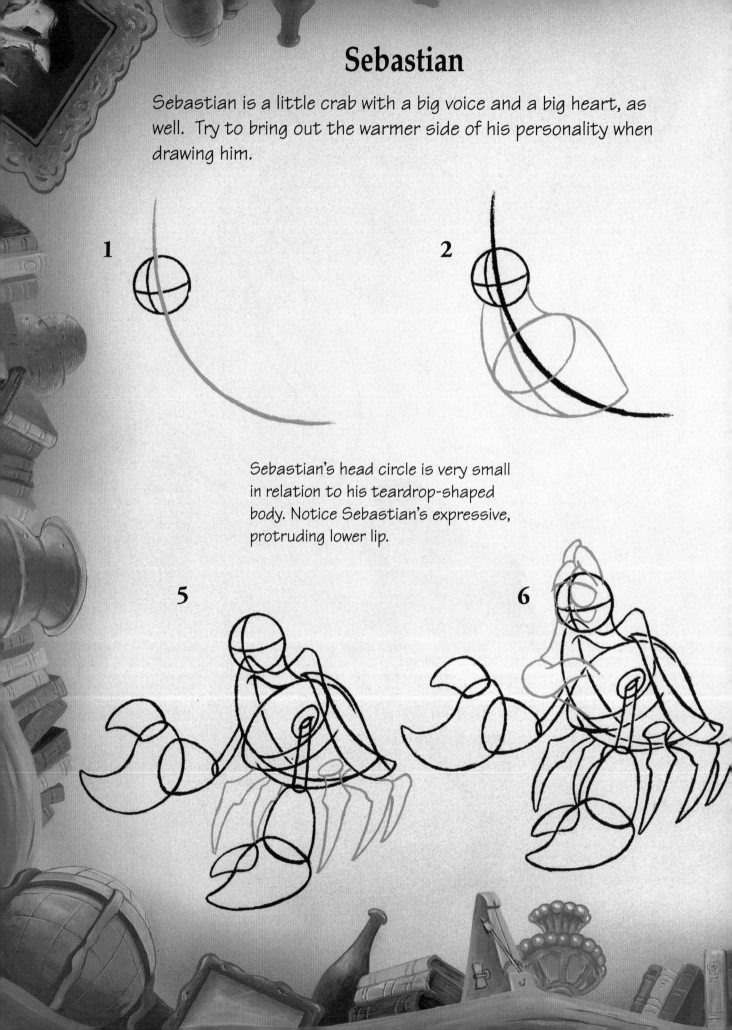

1

2

Sebastian's head circle is very small in relation to his teardrop-shaped body. Notice Sebastian's expressive, protruding lower lip.

5

6

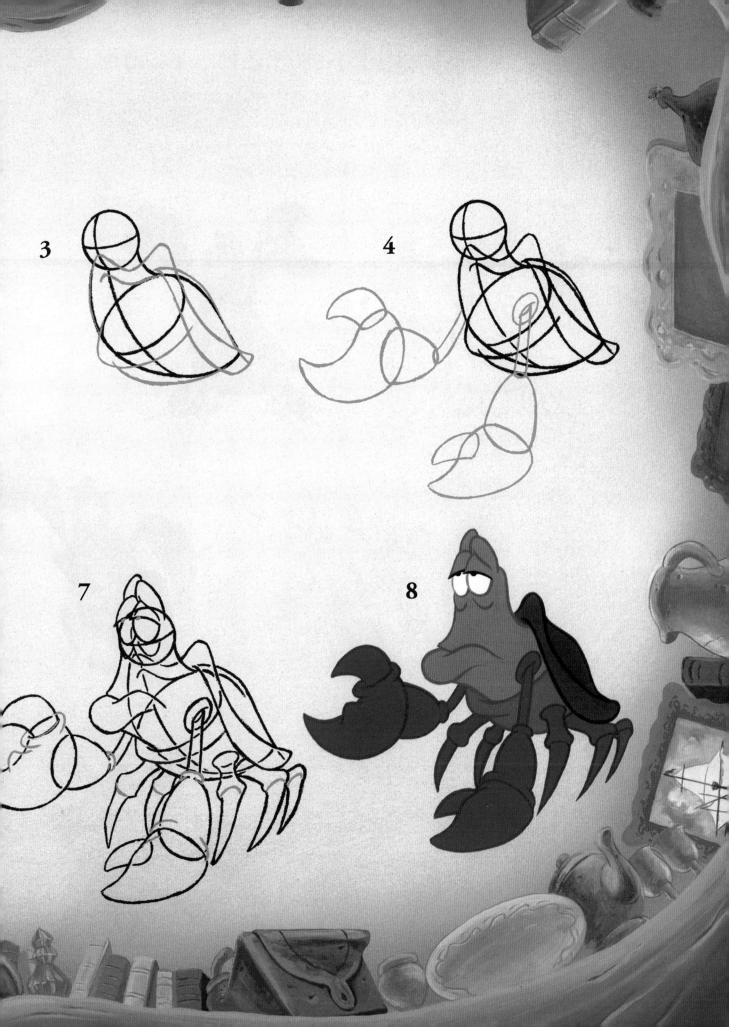

3

4

7

8

Sebastian's Poses and Expressions

When drawing Sebastian in action, notice that his hard shell
does not change shape. It is his flexible face that can be
exaggerated to show movement. Try this squash-and-stretch
technique when drawing Sebastian in action.

happy

showing off

fearful

proud

doubtful

singing

bowing

Flounder Three-Quarter View

Flounder's spunk and vulnerability are the qualities that make him so memorable. Use this three-quarter view to show all the depth of his chubby cheeks and oval nose.

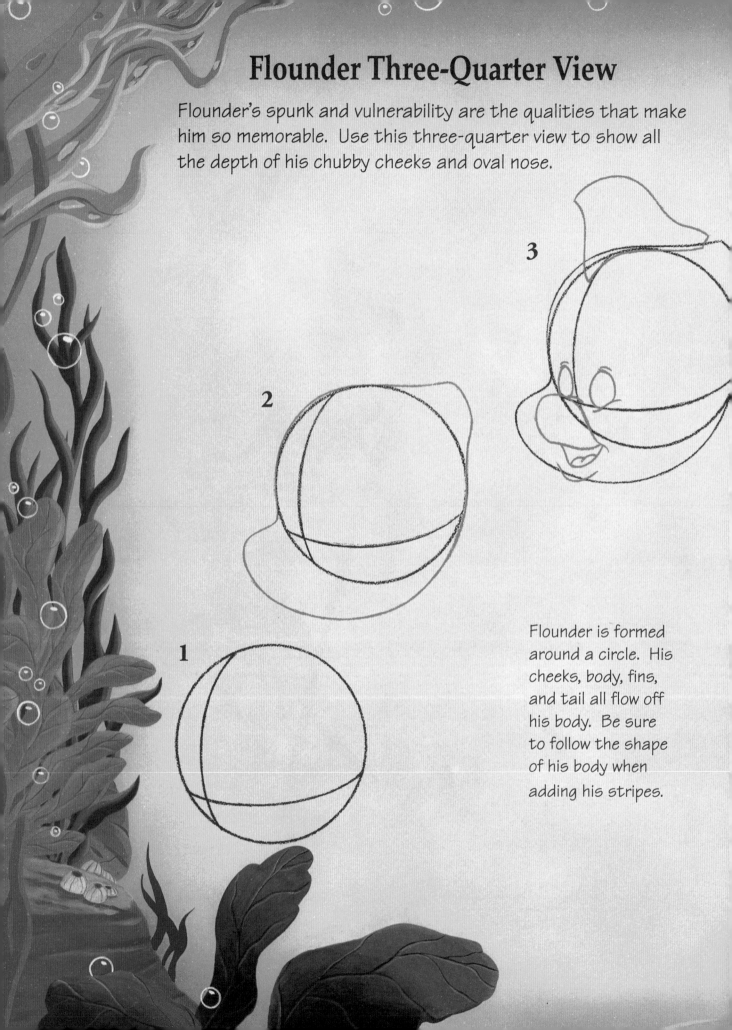

3

2

1

Flounder is formed around a circle. His cheeks, body, fins, and tail all flow off his body. Be sure to follow the shape of his body when adding his stripes.

4

5

6

Flounder's Poses and Expressions

Since Flounder doesn't have any limbs to draw, he is limited to simple arcs of action. However, his face can show a wide variety of emotions. Here are some of the different ways he can be drawn.

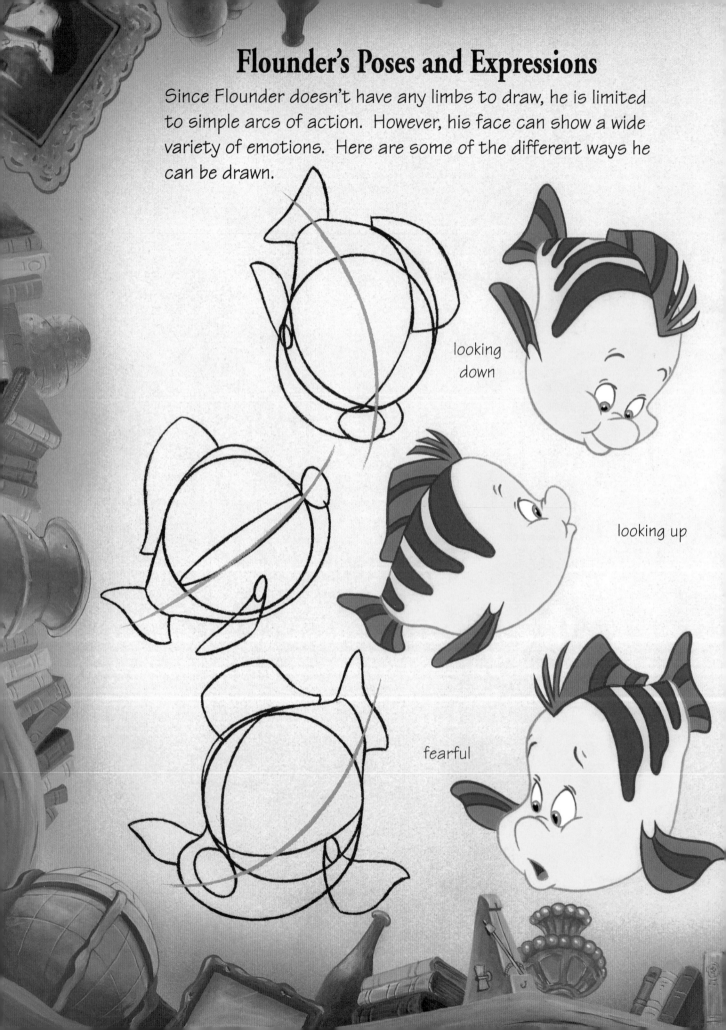

looking down

looking up

fearful

back view

happy

angry

Ursula Three-Quarter View

Ursula is basically constructed of simple shapes. Her six legs can be used either to propel her or to act as extra arms. All six are not always visible.

The top half of Ursula's body is smaller and more angular than the bottom half.

6

The legs should appear to join together underneath Ursula's wide body.

7

Ursula's Poses and Expressions

Ursula's gestures and expressions are dramatic and exaggerated. She is composed of circular shapes that you can squash and stretch to animate her.

furious

fearful

joyful

greedy

conniving

scheming

Scuttle Standing

Scuttle is overweight and scruffy. Now that you have learned to draw his head, you can move on to drawing his full body.

1

2

Scuttle's back is a concave curve, while his chest and lower body protrude in a convex curve.

3

Eric's Head

Of all the characters from *The Little Mermaid*, Eric's proportions are closest to those of an actual human. Here's how to draw his face.

1

Eric has a strong, angular jaw and chinline.

3

2

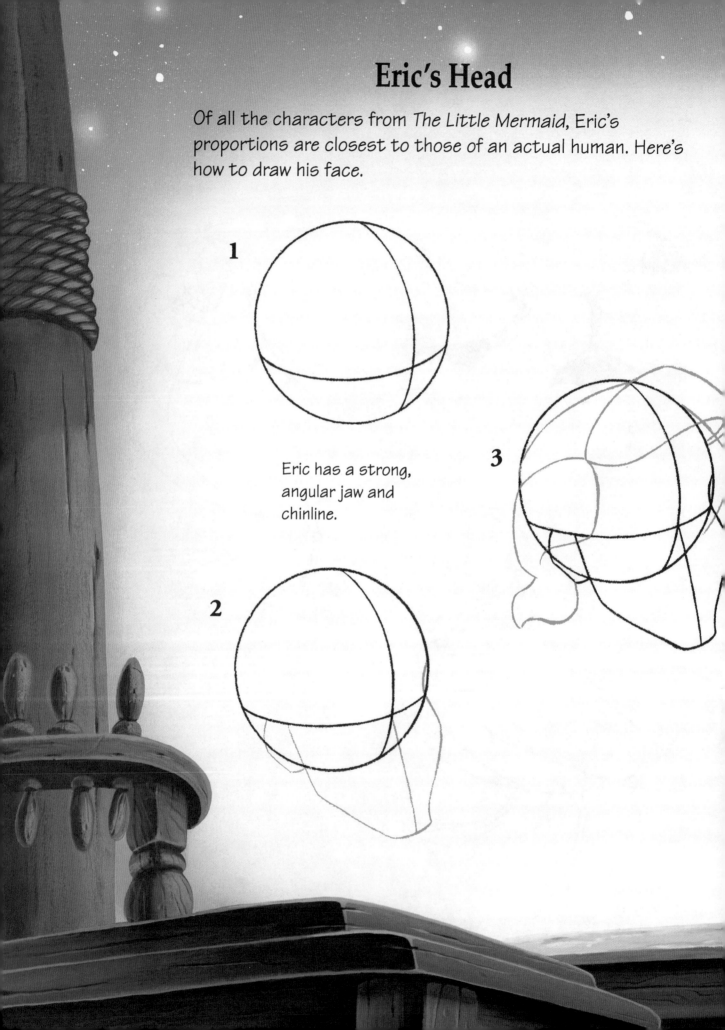

The top of Eric's head
is flatter than the
construction ball of
his head.

5

4

6

Eric Standing

After you have practiced drawing Eric's head and face, you are ready to move on to his body. He's a prince, so be sure he stands proudly.

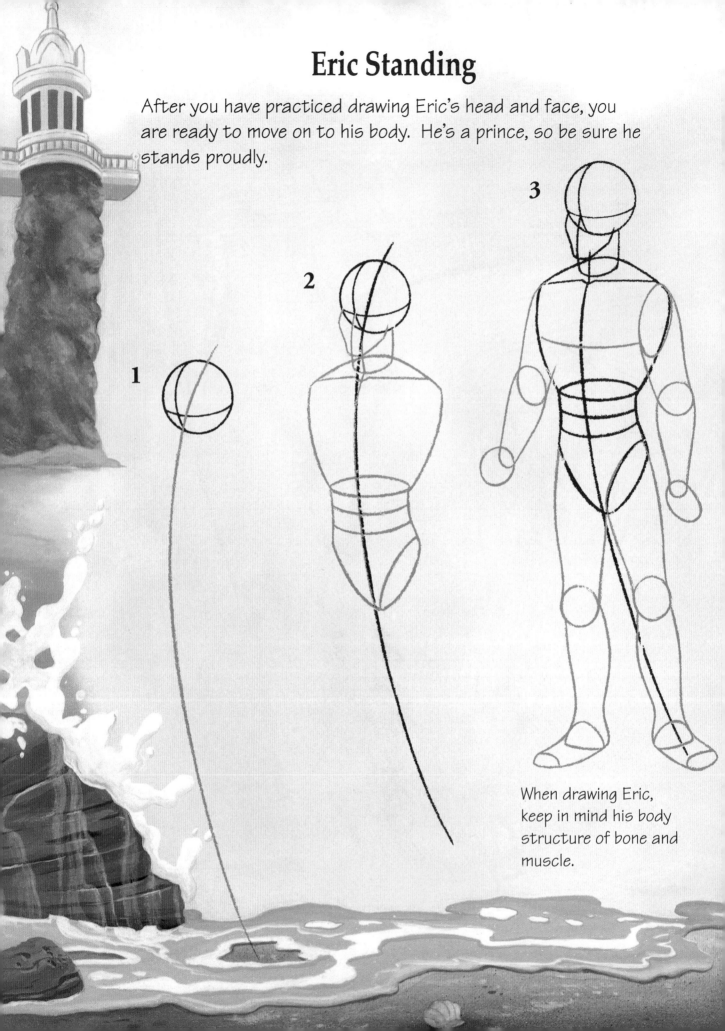

1

2

3

When drawing Eric, keep in mind his body structure of bone and muscle.

4

5

6

sure to add details
Eric's clothing such
fabric folds and
eases.

Winnie the Pooh

Designed and Illustrated by the Disney Publishing
Creative Development Staff

Getting Started

The first thing you'll need is a pencil with a good eraser. Lots of times when artists draw characters, they make extra lines to help them figure out where to put things like noses and ears and whiskers. If you use a pencil, you can erase these lines when your drawing is finished.

Notice the blue lines and the black lines in this sketch of Pooh's head. Throughout the section, each new step will be in blue. All the lines you've drawn before will be in black.

Did you know that drawing a circle is almost always the first step in drawing someone's head?

Before you begin, practice drawing circles. These will help you later when you start drawing your favorite characters.

fter you learn to draw Winnie the
ooh and all his friends, you'll want
 color them. For that you can use
elt-tip markers, crayons, colored
encils, or paints.

How Tall Is Pooh?

Christopher Robin

Winnie the Pooh

Piglet

Owl

Rabbit

...ake a close look at how the characters compare to one another. Some are ...ll; some are short; some are just about the same height. It's important to ...member this when you draw characters together—you wouldn't want Piglet ...look taller than Pooh!

Gopher   Eeyore

Tigger   Kanga and Roo

Winnie the Pooh

Drawing Pooh's Face

Pooh is a bear of little brain and big tummy. He has a one-food mind when it comes to honey. But he is also a good friend to Piglet and a perfect pal for "doing nothing" with Christopher Robin. Pooh has a simple sweetness to him that goes beyond the honey stuck to his paws!

How do you draw Pooh's ears?

Too pointy!

Too round!

Pooh's nose is a soft triangle.

Just right!

Sometimes Disney artists look in the mirror to see how to draw certain expressions. If Pooh were drawing a picture of himself, he'd have a perfect model for a giggling bear!

Step 1

Draw a circle. Then draw two lines crossed in the middle of the circle.

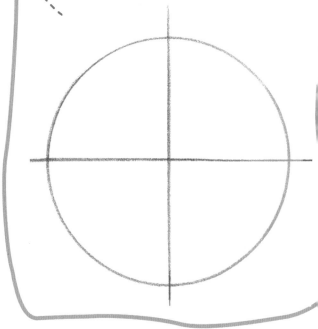

Step 4

Now add his smile.

Step 2

Add Pooh's ears, eyes, and chin. Don't forget his eyebrows!

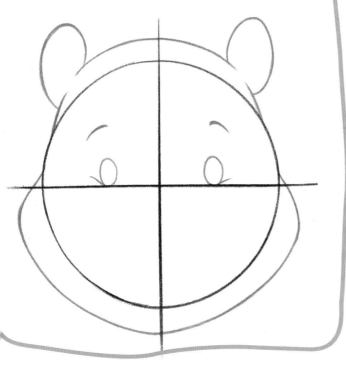

Step 3

Use the crossed lines to help you figure out where to draw Pooh's nose.

Step 5

Carefully erase the guidelines and clean up the drawing.

Step 6

Now color your picture!

Winnie the Pooh

Drawing Pooh's Body

Pooh's toes point in a little.

Keep ears apart in profile.

Shirt is loose fittin

Feet are soft and pliable to indicate toe area.

Step 1

Draw a circle for the head. Then add a pear shape below it for his body.

Step 2

Add Pooh's arms and legs.

Step 3

Use the blue lines to figure out where to put Pooh's eyes, nose, mouth, and shir

Piglet thinks the silly old bear is a wonderful friend.

Pooh is about 2½ heads high.

Pooh can have a little thumb if he needs to grab something.

Pooh's arms are almost the same length as his legs.

Step 4

Add sleeves and a collar to Pooh's shirt.

Step 5

You can erase the extra lines when you finish your picture.

Step 6

Now color your drawing!

Tigger

Drawing Tigger's Face

Tigger surely is one of a kind in the Hundred-Acre Wood. He's a good bouncing buddy for little Roo, but his springy style bowls over the others. Tigger is always sure of "what tiggers do best," even before he does something. But perhaps the really "wonderful thing" about Tigger is the bounce he brings to everyone around him.

Step 1

Use the crossed lines to help figure out where to draw Tigger's ears.

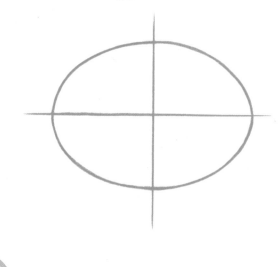

Tigger's ears are triangles about as wide as his nose.

When Tigger smiles, his eyes are single lines.

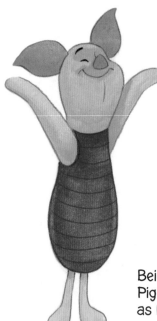

Being a very small animal, Piglet isn't always able to jump as high as his friend Tigger.

Step 4

Use curved lines to add Tigger's stripes and whiskers.

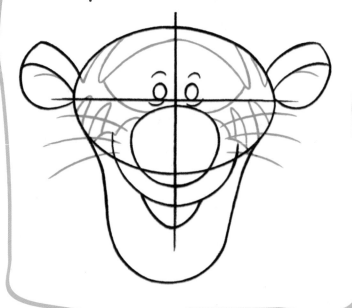

Step 2

Tigger's ears point up and out. Don't forget to draw Tigger's big chin.

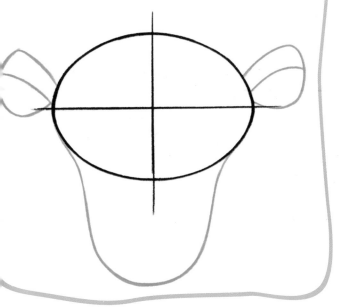

Step 3

Add Tigger's eyes and large nose. Then draw his big grin!

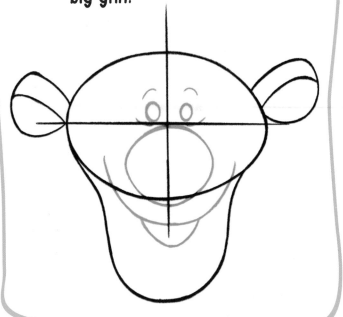

Step 5

Erase your guidelines and clean up the drawing.

Step 6

Color your picture of Tigger!

Tigger

Drawing Tigger's Body

Step 1

Tigger's body is a long oval with a short oval on top.

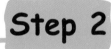

Step 2

Tigger's arms are much longer than his legs.

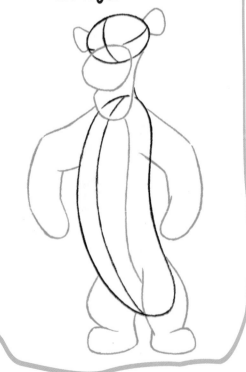

Step 3

The stripe pattern on Tigger's body varies. Use a mixture of large and small stripes.

His tail squishes when he bounces.

Step 4

Erase the construction lines and clean up the drawing.

Tigger's body is shaped like a banana.

Step 5

Color your picture!

Poor Eeyore always seems to be losing his tail. He can't even imagine what it must be like to have a springy tail like Tigger's that never falls off, even with the bounciest of bounces.

Piglet

Drawing Piglet's Head

Piglet is a very small animal. He is little enough to be swept away by a leaf and timid enough to be scared by Pooh's stories of "jagulars." His eyebrows and mouth usually show how he's feeling.

Piglet's head is peanut-shaped.

Make sure his ears don't point toward each other or he'll appear to have horns.

Being a small and timid animal, Piglet is often comforted by the strong and wise Christopher Robin.

Step 1

Draw your circle, then the crossed lines.

Step 4

Add floppy ears and a chubby cheek.

Step 2

Draw Piglet's long face with a point at the bottom.

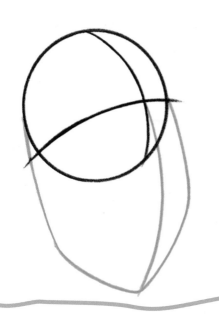

Step 3

Add Piglet's eyes, nose, and mouth along the crossed lines.

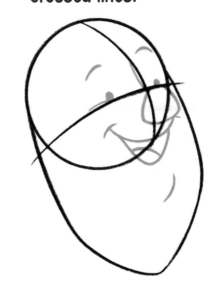

Step 5

Erase the construction lines and clean up the drawing.

Step 6

Now color the picture!

Piglet

Drawing Piglet's Body

Piglet is 2½ heads tall without ears.

His arm and hand can wrap around objects to grab them.

Step 1

The head is a circle, and the body is shaped like a jelly bean.

Step 4

Add the floppy ears, chubby cheek, and body stripes.

Step 5

Carefully erase the construction lines and clean up the drawing.

Step 2

Draw the neck and feet.

Step 3

Add the eyes, nose, and mouth along the crossed lines.

Step 6

Now color your drawing!

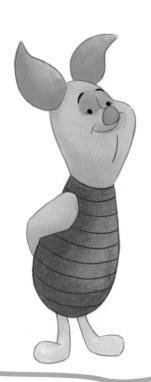

Roo and Piglet have something in common: they're both quite small. In fact, Roo happens to fit perfectly inside Kanga's pouch.

Eyore

Drawing Eyore's Head

Things are always looking down for Eeyore. With a tail that comes loose and a house that falls down, he's always ready for things to go wrong. Still, Eeyore manages to smile once in a while, even though he's almost always gloomy.

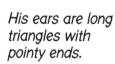

His ears are long triangles with pointy ends.

His mane falls forward.

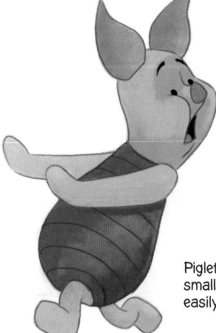

Piglet, being a very small animal, is easily frightened.

Step 1

Draw a circle with crossed lines for the head.

Step 4

Little curved lines around Eeyore's eyes make him look sad.

Step 2

Then add a shape like a sack for his nose.

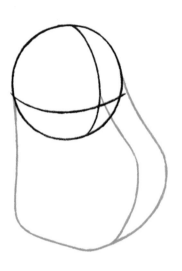

Step 3

Eeyore's ears, eyes, and eyebrows usually droop downward.

Step 5

Erase the construction lines and clean up the drawing.

Step 6

Color your picture of Eeyore!

Eeyore
Drawing Eeyore's Body

Step 1

Draw a circle for his head and a big pillow shape for his body.

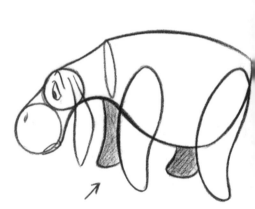

Keep Eeyore's legs simple since he's a stuffed animal.

Step 2

Now draw his ears, legs, and tail. Then add his shaggy mane.

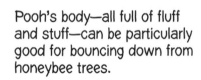

Pooh's body—all full of fluff and stuff—can be particularly good for bouncing down from honeybee trees.

Step 3

Add a bow to his tail to help cheer him up.

Normally, his tail hangs straight down, but it can fly up in a heavy wind.

Step 4

Erase the construction lines and clean up the drawing.

Step 5

Now color your picture!

Kanga and Roo

Drawing Kanga's & Roo's Bodies

Kanga is kind of like the mother to everyone in the Hundred-Acre Wood—but especially to her own little boy, Roo. Did you know that if you put Kanga's and Roo's names together they spell "KANGAROO"? And that is, of course, the kind of animal they are.

Step 1

Kanga has a small, round head atop a body shaped like a kidney bean. Roo also has a round head—but it's even smaller.

Keep hands glovelike.

Keep feet large and soft.

For Tigger, bouncing is fun, fun, fun! Roo agrees with his pal and tries to imitate Tigger's bouncing whenever he can.

Step 2

Add Kanga's ears, arms, legs, and tail. Then draw the details of her face. Don't forget Roo's face, too.

Step 3

Draw in the details of Kanga's and Roo's bodies.

Step 4

Carefully erase the construction lines and clean up the drawing.

Step 5

Now color the picture!

Christopher Robin

Drawing Christopher Robin's Head

Christopher Robin is really just a child, but Pooh and his friends always come to him for help. Whether Eeyore has lost his tail or Pooh is stuck in Rabbit's doorway, Christopher Robin usually has an idea to solve the problem. When things turn out just right, he's always ready to celebrate with a parade or a party.

Step 1

Draw a circle for his head.

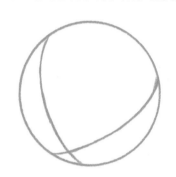

Show a few hairs on the crown of his head. Keep his neck thin to emphasize his large head.

Christopher Robin is about 4 heads tall, or roughly twice as tall as Pooh.

Step 4

Add his nose and understanding smile.

His shirt is not usually tucked in.

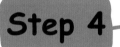

His pants are simple and loose-fitting.

His right sock is always falling down.

His shoes are flat with almost no heel.

When his mouth is open, you can see his top row of teeth.

Keep the eyes small.

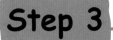

No "quotation mark" eyes.

Step 2

Add his cheeks and chin.

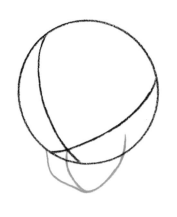

Step 3

Add his hair and kind eyes.

Step 5

Erase the construction lines and clean up the drawing.

Step 6

Color your picture.

Rabbit

Drawing Rabbit's Head

Rabbit is very organized, right down to the neat rows of vegetables in his garden. He can be fussy and easily frustrated. Still, Rabbit is a good friend to the others—just as they are good friends to him.

His nose is not a circle. It has definite planes.

Both ears come to a point.

He has large, fuzzy eyebrows.

He has a definite shoulder.

His furry chest sticks out.

His tail resembles a large cotton ball.

Rabbit's wrists are thin.

He has three toes.

Step 1

Draw a circle for the head.

Step 4

Add the whiskers and fur.

Make sure the point on the back of Rabbit's head is at the bottom, not the middle.

No!

Yes!

Step 2

Draw his nose and the back of his head.

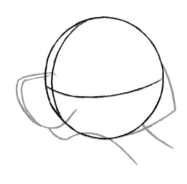

Step 3

Draw in the details of his head and his ears.

Step 5

Erase the construction lines and clean up the drawing.

Step 6

Now color your picture.

Coloring Styles

Some people like to color their pictures with pencils or crayons. Of course, Pooh wouldn't mind coloring everything with bright yellow honey, but we recommend paints for a more finished look and chalky pastels for a fuzzier look. Whatever you decide, remember to use your imagination and have fun!

Even Eeyore likes bright, colorful crayons (but he wouldn't want you to bother with much more than gray on his account).

The Hundred-Acre Wood

Pooh's House Pooh's cozy little home usually has lots of empty honeypots right outside its front door.

The Path There's always a shaded grassy place to sit and rest on a walk through the Hundred-Acre Wood.

Enchanted Spot

This is one of Christopher Robin's and Pooh's favorite spots to sit and, well, do nothing . . . together, of course.

Rabbit's House

The fussy and orderly Rabbit always has his plants labeled and his laundry neatly hung on a line to dry.

Eeyore's Place

"Not much of a home, but good enough for the likes of me," says Eeyore.

Kanga and Roo's

Anyone's welcome to drop in for tea at Kanga and Roo's.

Good Luck

Despite the many differences among
all the characters who inhabit the
Hundred-Acre Wood, they bear one
thing in common: they're happiest
when they're together.